8-Bit Apocalypse

THE NEW BIZARRO AUTHOR SERIES

PRESENTS

8-Bit Apocalypse

Amanda Billings

Eraserhead Press

Portland, OR

ERASERHEAD PRESS
205 NE BRYANT
PORTLAND, OR 97211

WWW.ERASERHEADPRESS.COM

ISBN: 978-1-62105-124-4

Printed in the USA.

Editor's Note:

Welcome to the New Bizarro Author Series. This is Amanda Billing's first book. I first "met" her when I published a story of hers in my literary journal, *Bust Down the Door and Eat All the Chickens* (which is now defunct). It was called "Guess What" and it was about a board game called *Guess What?* whose boards come alive and attack people. The writing was fantastic, so I was psyched when Amanda contacted me about possibly writing a book for the series. Amanda decided to write a book about a giant Atari cartridge coming alive, causing various old games to play in the real world, which of course results in disaster (perhaps inanimate objects becoming sentient and EVIL is Amanda's thing). And since Amanda is a classic gaming enthusiast and has actually attended a Donkey Kong tournament, I thought she was the perfect author for the book. I've even seen a photo with her and Walter Day, the founder of Twin Galaxies, which is an organization that keeps track of world records in video gaming.

Now let's talk about the series: it's designed to test the waters for new bizarro authors to see if they have what it takes to find a readership. It's up to you as far as whether or not Eraserhead Press will be publishing more of Amanda's books in the future. To succeed, she must sell several hundred copies of this book over the next year. So if you like this book, I encourage you to tell your friends about it and write a review (particularly for Amazon).

Thanks so much for giving this book a chance. I hope you enjoy it as much as I enjoyed editing it.

~~Bradley Sands

For Brett, my arcade hero

Chapter One

In Which We Meet Our Hero

Jimmy Toledo is having his favorite fantasy. I am in the hydro-massage tube at the mall food court, Jimmy thinks to himself. I walked right up to those Korean women in the fake lab coats and gave them my credit card and they giggled and locked me in this pod. I've been suctioned inside tight black plastic and every inch of my body is being pounded by hot hard streams of water. I am floating in black space in the mall food court and these women know that I'm not squeezing in some ten minute jerk off session before getting my Auntie Anne's. Oh no. I'm getting a full body factory reset. I am being reborn.

Jimmy is actually lying in a plastic sky tube suspended fifteen feet off the floor of a Chuck E. Cheese in downtown Denver. He is an assistant party planner at Chuck E. Cheese and there is a large puddle of someone else's vomit a half foot from his head and the plastic of the tube flooring presses his nose into a pleasantly uncomfortable angle. He hears the first mole sounds of a child approaching him in the sky tube and turns up the volume on his phone. Through his earbuds he can hear the lisping whispers of a Russian woman describing her closet organizational strategies in broken English. Jimmy is subscribed to many YouTube whisper video channels, more often than not simply listening to the whispering voices while the video plays unwatched in his pants pocket. This Russian woman's soft voice makes Jimmy feel connected to her in a way that makes him connected to all women, like her descriptions of her closet are some kind of universal chant that connects into all forms of feminine love and attention.

Jimmy volunteered to be on sky tube oopsie duty today because he needs this sky tube fantasy time in order to control himself during the monthly video game maintenance visits that reset all the high scores. The last maintenance visit had been especially difficult as Jimmy had managed to keep his 12,000 point score on the bottom of the *Ms. Pac-Man* rankings for two weeks. He had planned on punching the maintenance man in the face, and then thought about kicking him instead while the maintenance worker was squatting down by the machines, and then thought maybe dumping a cup of soda on his head would work better because that could look like an accident. Jimmy ended up just spilling some soda near the maintenance man's feet while trying not to cry as his *Ms. Pac-Man* score was erased. The maintenance man had looked up at Jimmy and Jimmy thought that the man must know who Jimmy was, but the maintenance man had no idea who Jimmy was, which was perhaps worse than being recognized.

But that was a whole month ago, and the maternal whispers in broken English and the hydro-massage fantasy have pushed it so far away that score rankings on the beat up arcade games cannot touch him. The Russian whisper video he is listening to gives him a non-sexual erection, and the hydro-massage full body factory reset fantasy gives him a non-sexual erection, and he is so relaxed that he almost can't smell the pizza vomit cut with foamy root beer pooling half a foot from his head. "Weenter shurts go left side of closet," the Russian woman says. The water burns his skin even through the plastic casing and the Korean women in the fake lab coats admire Jimmy's dedication to starting a new life. He is so brave, they say to each other.

The mole-child has reached Jimmy and is bashing her head into the bottom of Jimmy's greasy rubber-soled work shoes. "Move!" she screams.

"This section is closed," Jimmy says without lifting his head. The Russian woman is describing her casual and semi-formal dresses. "Green dress with flowers." Jimmy knows the video by heart, can see her glossy fingernails delicately tracing the outline of the printed flowers. "Bloo dress. Lassy dress for chorch." The girl rams her head into Jimmy's shoes again.

"I hate you!" the little girl screams, and Jimmy can hear her, and his hydro-massage fantasy is very hard to maintain at this point. Jimmy wonders what his life would be like if things had gone differently, if he was married and had a child like this one to take to Chuck E. Cheese, although he would never take his child to this particular Chuck E. Cheese because it is one of the lowest-ranked Chuck E. Cheeses in the Western United States in both safety and customer satisfaction. Jimmy lifts his head up and watches as the beast child begins crawling over his shoes, digging her knees into his legs, and punching him in the ass. Jimmy is not sure if he would like the alternate life with the wife and the child, but he does know it would be better than his current life, in which his fantasy time in the sky tube by the pizza vomit will undoubtedly be the best part of his day. He turns up on one side, dumping the child off of his back, and gently kicks her down the sky tube shaft behind him. His non-sexual erection is gone and the space between this month and last month is gone and the pizza root beer vomit is still pooling in front of him.

Jimmy comes down out of the sky tube with soiled vomit rags stuffed into a Chuck E. Cheese takeout bag. His manager is pulling a drowning child out of the ball pit with a broom handle and whacks Jimmy with the broom handle once the child has been freed. "What the fuck takes you so long up there?" he says. "Sanders here can clean up a shit-puke combo in five minutes. That's why he's been the oopsie regional leader three times in a row."

"Three times, dickweed," Sanders says as he speed-walks past the two of them to a birthday party pant-wetting. Jimmy isn't jealous of the oopsie regional leader title necessarily, but he does like the idea of having his name read out loud at the quarterly regional meeting and getting a five dollar gift card to Cold Stone Creamery for lying in a vomit tube and listening to whisper videos.

"You used to be a champion, son," his manager says, and Jimmy feels a thick surge of shame stab his stomach. "What the hell happened to you?"

Jimmy's manager says that to everyone, including some of the children who become trapped in the ball pit, but to the best of Jimmy's knowledge, Jimmy is the only actual former champion of anything currently employed at this Chuck E. Cheese location. Jimmy doesn't readily share this knowledge—that he was a child prodigy in the arcades, that he is currently thirty-six and about to climb into a Chuck E. Cheese rat suit of his own volition, that he is currently champion of nothing, not even regional oopsie clean up. I *am* a dickweed, Jimmy thinks as he heads to the supply closet to change, and the Korean women at the mall food court are never going to think that I am brave, and children are routinely able to beat my high scores.

Jimmy takes off his pants and pulls on the communal under-rat-suit gym shorts, which are awkwardly stained and tight across his thighs, and steps into the rat legs, which feel slightly damp. He cannot listen to his whisper videos in the rat suit because children are constantly hugging and kicking him when he wears the suit, which would be awkward with his non-sexual erection and which would also generally destroy the safe feeling that comes with women describing mundane things in soft voices. He inserts his arms into the rat arms of the suit, then fumbles with the back zipper with thick, useless rat fingers. He puts the rat head on and waddles out of the supply closet toward the birthday party on the other end of the dark orange and purple Chuck E. Cheese floor. Jimmy imagines that he is an astronaut chosen for an especially hostile mission because his co-astronauts all realize that Jimmy sucks.

Chapter Two

Our Hero's Sordid Past

Jimmy Toledo's father is screaming at him from across the crowded arcade floor. "I won't love you unless you win," Jimmy's father says, which is what he always says to encourage his son's success. It is 1983 and Jimmy has just turned seven years old. He is standing on a wooden milk crate in front of a *Donkey Kong* cabinet vying to be the first American of any age to play the game from start to finish. Rumors that a top Japanese player defeated the game have been moving through the competitive gaming circuit for the past few weeks. While no one can agree upon just what happened at this fabled ending—Jumpman beating Donkey Kong to death with his hammer, Pauline voluntarily leaving Jumpman for Donkey Kong—the message that *Donkey Kong* is beatable, whether true or not, has sent extra electricity through gaming competitions nationwide.

Jimmy has already surpassed 800,000 points, a personal record that would also put him at the top of the American record if it weren't for Clyde Dryval, Jimmy's twenty-two-year-old competition who is managing to keep up with Jimmy's pace better than anyone had anticipated. Jimmy's father has a lot of money riding on the game, which he indicates to Jimmy by screaming, "I've got a lot of money riding on this game, you little shit," at regular intervals. Jimmy's mother is not there, as she didn't want to make the flight out from their hometown of Denver to Houston, where this particular tournament is being held, and because unlike Jimmy's father, who will love Jimmy if he wins, Jimmy's mother will remain indifferent in her affections regardless.

Jimmy had been a video game prodigy from birth, mastering *Pong* before he could walk, defeating arcade ports for the Atari 2600 as a toddler, and putting up previously unheard of high scores by the age of four. Jimmy's video game intelligence quotient was tested at 230 at the age of five, landing him on the front page of the Denver Post's local section and the back page Stories of the World sections of several other papers. Jimmy was able to see the patterns in 8-bit space alien attacks and elevating platforms the way that others picked out startled horse faces in repeating wood grain patterns on cheap doors. Jimmy's genius, though great, was confined to his Atari 2600 and his chubby-handed grip on the joystick; though not slow in other areas of his young life, he was decidedly average. Jimmy's father, a man who could not be described as intelligent but who could be described as someone capable of selling his son's childhood in the name of profit, started Jimmy off in local hustles and self-organized tournaments before connecting with larger national tournaments offering cash prizes and under the table gambling opportunities.

As the tournaments Jimmy's father entered him in became increasingly mainstream, Jimmy found himself moving from the back rooms in darkened bars to playing in arcades where children cordially associated with other children and occasionally someone's mother would come by to watch. "Winners don't have friends," Jimmy's father would say when Jimmy asked. "And winners don't have mothers either. Just play the fucking game." But Jimmy was increasingly intrigued by the interactions he saw around him—amicable, even loving interactions—and as he stands on his milk crate in 1983, instinctively tracking the barrels as they roll from Donkey Kong's angry fists and listening to his father tell him that he won't love Jimmy unless Jimmy wins, Jimmy wonders if that's really true.

Jimmy has been playing *Donkey Kong* for over an hour and a half and his feet are sore and he is hungry and has to pee but he is on level 21, which is further than he has ever gotten before, and Clyde Dryval is matching him stage for stage and Jimmy is on his last life. They are getting close to the end of the game. Jimmy can feel it behind his eyes, a tingling through his brain and down his back as he follows the familiar path of Jumpman's steps up the ladder. It can't be long now.

The last stage of level 21 begins, the rivet stage, where Jumpman must remove rivets supporting Donkey Kong's metal scaffolding while avoiding the unintelligent but fast moving fireballs that bounce between the platforms. The fireballs spawn on the right-hand side of the screen and sprint toward Jimmy's Jumpman, but Jimmy knows the pattern he needs to follow to maximize points and minimize danger—up ladder, pull rivet, up ladder, pull rivet, up ladder, skip rivet—fast enough to match the pacing that increases with each subsequent level. Jimmy's Jumpman races up the next ladder, the fireball waiting at the top is frozen in place (unusual, though not unheard of), but as he waits a half-beat for the fireball to bounce away or chase him down the ladder, Jimmy sees the fireball stay in place, blocking his path as the other fireballs gather around Jumpman's feet with alarming speed. Jimmy is trapped on the ladder and must choose between moving up and almost certainly colliding with the waiting fireball above him or moving down into a pulsing pit of flames. If he moves up, there is a chance the fireball would move back into its high-speed bouncing pattern and jump out of the way. If he moves down, there is a chance he could grab a fire-crushing hammer before getting swarmed and make it out alive. He has one-tenth of a second to decide.

Another player at this tournament has lost his last Jumpman at 756,000 points, and his girlfriend or possibly sister is comforting him instead of making threats about withholding food. The girlfriend or possibly sister is touching the defeated *Donkey Kong* player on the shoulder and Jimmy catches the glint of the girlfriend or possibly sister's pink nail polish in the low arcade light as her fingers rise and fall at random, beautiful intervals and Jimmy jerks his joystick up and straight into the fireball, which did not fall back into its pattern and did not move out of the way.

Jimmy hears his father yelling and Jimmy starts to cry because the non-patterned shoulder squeezing is ringing through his seven-year-old head where the game pattern that never reappeared should be and in the absence of the game pattern making any sense he thinks that this simple touch is the only thing he has ever wanted. The girlfriend or possibly sister points to Jimmy and says, "Hey, look, that kid's crying. What a baby." And Jimmy's competitor Clyde Dryval starts laughing and Jimmy's dad starts laughing and everyone is laughing and calling Jimmy a baby.

Clyde Dryval beats the stage that Jimmy died on and everyone stops laughing and stops paying attention to Jimmy as Clyde Dryval's Jumpman runs forward into the first stage of level 22, jumps over a barrel, climbs up a ladder, and dies. Everyone starts clapping.

"But you just died," Jimmy says, wiping at his face.

"You can't beat this game," Clyde Dryval says. "It just ends. God, what did you think happened?" Jimmy had thought that Jumpman and Pauline would run away together, and that maybe Pauline would touch Jumpman gently on the shoulder like the girlfriend or possibly sister, but Jimmy does not share this with Clyde Dryval because Jimmy's father is dragging him out of the arcade. When Jimmy and his father fly back to Denver the following day, Jimmy's father drops him off at Jimmy's grandmother's house, where Jimmy will spend the rest of his childhood.

"Some people just use up all their special early," Jimmy's grandmother says to him as she tidies up around Jimmy's sprawled body on her living room floor. The vacuum nudges Jimmy's side and he is appreciative of the contact. "Seems like you're one of those people."

Jimmy eventually tries to play again, first on the Atari that his father will throw into his grandmother's bushes, and eventually on the cabinets at the local arcade, but he will never reach the *Donkey Kong* kill screen or come close to his former high scores. His preternatural pattern recognition is broken. He has been touched by Fear and Doubt, and worst still, a trembling sort of Hope, which has proved impossible for such an otherwise average boy to shake.

Chapter Three

A History Lesson with Grave Consequences

While Jimmy is playing at the tournament in Houston that will shape the rest of his life, a convoy of trucks haul waste to a remote garbage dump in New Mexico. These trucks contain over one million unsold copies of *E.T. the Extraterrestrial*, an Atari 2600 game that will be remembered as one of the worst video games to ever exist. The game play consists primarily of falling into large, tedious holes in the ground, making the game's ultimate resting place in a similarly inescapable pit both poetic and a useful tax write-off at what is the start of Atari's downfall.

The E.T. cartridges have been crushed and encased in cement to ensure an easy burial despite the overall quantity of the haul, but a few extra cases from the Atari warehouse in El Paso have also been included in the truck caravan as part of a larger, preemptive housecleaning measure, shoved into the truck at the last minute without being properly crushed and sealed. These other cases include defective Atari 2600 systems and copies of more popular arcade ports like *Frogger*, *Centipede*, and *Space Invaders*, most of which were returned to Atari for trivial reasons: the games were harder to control than their arcade counterparts, the games' programming seemed off, etc. One particularly nasty batch was returned with complaints that the game remembered the player's progress and refused to start fresh from the easiest stages, as if the games had a choice in the matter.

Aside from being advised that the Bally Astrocade console might be more their speed, the customers returning these items were given full refunds while the games and systems were sent off to the El Paso warehouse for storage.

Whatever problems the games enclosed in these crates may have had, they're heading to the dump now, where they'll spend the next twenty years nestled in New Mexican soil irradiated with decades of regional nuclear testing.

Chapter Four

A Giant Flying Atari Cartridge Disrupts Our Hero's Shift

Jimmy has a hard time hearing the explosions and screaming through the large stuffed rat head he is wearing, but he can feel the floor jolt and vibrate through his costumed feet and has turned his rat eyes toward the Chuck E. Cheese front door. He had just attempted to lead a birthday party through a round of the Hokey Pokey, which resulted in pepperoni being flung at Jimmy while he danced. Now that he has stopped, the children scream for him to dance again. Some of the parents drinking 3.2 beer at the Chuck E. Cheese bar look up and contemplate whether it is worth investigating what must be large-scale destruction outside or if it would be better to just let these potential final moments of their lives pass side by side with strangers in a poorly lit bar at a children's pizzeria.

Jimmy is waddling his rat legs toward the tinted glass entrance doors without realizing what he is doing. As he pushes the doors open a chain of light rail cars that have been ripped off their tracks go streaking past the Chuck E. Cheese and around a street corner one block up. In the distance Jimmy sees a large black shape rising up above the buildings in a normally empty part of the skyline, occupying the outdoor pedestrian shopping area of the 16th Street Mall. Dust and smoke billow up around the edges of the massive black object as if it has just crashed into the earth.

He begins running down the sidewalk toward it, ripping off his rat head and pawing at his zipper while he chugs forward. Panting with the greatest physical exertion he has experienced in weeks, he is forced to stop to fully disassemble the costume, and as he peels himself out of his damp rat pants and rests his black rubber-soled work shoes on the sidewalk a woman crossing the street calls Jimmy a pervert. Jimmy checks to make sure that he is still wearing the communal under-rat-suit gym shorts, as they sometimes get stripped off with the rat pants when removed with vigor, and as he looks down at his still-covered crotch the light rail caravan comes roaring past again and splits the woman crossing the street in two, severing her body at the waist and leaving her scowling face fixed on Jimmy as she dies. As blood and the partially processed contents of her digestive track spill onto the roadway, Jimmy feels a little sad that this woman's last moments were occupied with thoughts of him undressing on a street corner. Normally this scene would have been more unsettling for Jimmy and would have surely led to hours of contemplating What This All Means while internalizing the dead scowl on the woman's face, but there is a killer light rail train on the loose and explosions and screaming coming from around the black object's impact site that pull Jimmy's attention away. Whatever the large black block is, an alien invader, a foreign attack, Jimmy is compelled toward it in a way he hasn't felt in years—not even the lull of his whisper videos or the Korean women at the food court can compete with the pulsing draw that Jimmy feels toward this object, a feeling that brings him back to his perch on a milk crate so long ago. Even if he is cut in two before he arrives at the object, he won't die in a rat suit.

Chapter Five

In Which Our Hero Discovers a Real-Life Game of Centipede

Within a few blocks, Jimmy's sprint toward the 16th Street Mall is halted by an overturned police car, still smoking, and a group of fashionably-dressed twentysomethings watching videos on their cell phones with three police officers. One of the police officers is laughing and bleeding from a large red gash above his right eye. A girl in white shorts and strappy sandals and an oversized t-shirt says, "I think this is the best one of you," and the bleeding officer says, "Yes, totally," and as Jimmy approaches he sees that they are watching a video of the police car getting hit by the rogue light rail train and flipping up on the sidewalk with the bleeding officer inside.

"Are you okay?" Jimmy asks, breathing heavily, and the police officers and the twentysomethings all turn to look at him and he can see their eyes tracing the sweat stains on his Chuck E. Cheese work shirt with the large grinning skateboarding rat on the front. Someone holds their phone up and faces the camera lens at Jimmy and it makes the fake camera shutter sound and no one says anything. Jimmy says, "What's going on?" and the girl in the white shorts rolls her eyes like Jimmy is preventing her friends and these cops from going to an afternoon rooftop party and they're all going to have to wait for this sweaty unattractive guy to get hit by the light rail monster before they can do anything fun. Jimmy reaches his hand into his pocket and jiggles his earbuds across his fingertips and wonders if he could covertly start listening to his whisper videos while he talks with these intimidating people about why Denver is under attack.

"The giant flying black Atari thing came and crashed into the 16th Street Mall and started shooting people with lightning and controlling the light rail," White Shorts says. She brings up a video on her phone and hands it to Jimmy and Jimmy sees a giant flying Atari cartridge slam itself into the ground, crushing pedestrians and a few pigeons and a dog underneath it, and then it starts shaking and people are sort of screaming but also getting out their phones to take pictures, and then it starts blasting people with bolts of electricity and the *Centipede* game logo flickers on the massive black front of the cartridge like it's being lit up from within.

"It's a giant Atari game," Jimmy says.

"Obviously," White Shorts says. She grabs the phone back from him.

"Were you there? Did you film that?" Jimmy asks. White Shorts snorts.

"No, all those people are dead. Can you imagine though, being the first one to shoot and send out that video? Whoever it was is lucky they got it up so fast. A lot of people were able to Instagram before they were killed, though. Just get on Twitter. I can't believe you don't know what's happening." White Shorts looks back at her phone and laughs. "Someone just posted a pic of you," she says, and holds up her phone so that Jimmy can see the picture of him taken seconds before, sweating, slightly hunched over, with the caption, "What do you work at Chuck E. Cheese or something?" and the hashtag #whatdoyouworkatchuckecheeseorsomething. Jimmy pulls his earbuds out of his pocket but hesitates because he isn't sure if listening to a whisper video right now would make him feel calm or more awkward so he holds onto the earbuds like a tiny leash for his pants.

"Hey, we're on TV," the twentysomething who Instagrammed Jimmy says and he points up to the Sky Fox local news helicopter while watching a live feed of the helicopter on his phone. The police officers wave at the helicopter but nobody else does. Looking over the twentysomething's shoulder Jimmy can see the news helicopter's live feed playing on a cell phone screen. The camera zooms out and Jimmy sees several light rail trains wind through the city streets like a huge game of *Centipede*.

Jimmy slips his earbuds in and pulls out his phone to start up a whisper video and selects from his bookmarks a 43 minute video in which a Russian woman explains how to give a relaxing massage to a cat in great detail. Jimmy enjoys listening to this video in particular because the woman talks to the cat as if the cat is the listener, and Jimmy can easily allow himself to feel light female fingers raking through the imaginary fur on his imaginary haunches. The Russian woman whispers, "This is a good way to bond with animal," and Jimmy is still watching the aerial live feed of the Centipede light rails and tracing their zig zags across city blocks. Each light rail train snakes a path about seven or eight blocks wide as it winds away from the large Atari cartridge lodged in the 16th Street Mall, like each train is creating its own *Centipede* board, waiting for a player.

A group of armored vehicles pull up to the end of a block not far from Jimmy. The light rail that destroyed the police car turns onto the street with the armored vehicles and the armored vehicles begin firing on the Centipede train head-on with explosives. "What do you dream of as I touch?" the Russian woman asks, and for a moment Jimmy can feel his body under her fingers and can see the faces of the Korean woman smiling down on his relaxing cat shape.

The first car on the train buckles and jackknifes as the explosives hit, and the end two cars on the train flip forward and begin rolling. They crash into the armored vehicles, which jerk under the force of the impact but remain intact, and the overturned Centipede train twitches and spasms like an animal recently parted with its head.

"You can feel now my fingers unlocking knot between shoulder blades," the Russian woman murmurs. "The vibration of your purrs tickles my fingertips."

The Sky Fox live feed zooms out and shows the giant Atari cartridge send out a bolt of thick white lightning and electrocute a connected two-bus shuttle, which then begins to speed along the same path as the recently immobilized light rail centipede, replacing it. The sounds of car alarms and windows breaking and people screaming that have been spiking and falling from the surrounding city streets fade out and the whispers of the Russian woman fade out and Jimmy sees the Sky Fox live feed with the clarity of his seven-year-old prodigy mind. There are three *Centipede* boards being played, radiating out from the massive Atari game and repeating the same game screen over and over because no one is playing the role of the tiny side-scrolling gnome at the bottom of the screen.

"It's replaying the screen," Jimmy says. "It's replaying the screen because we're not following the rules. Someone's got to be the gnome."

"Someone's got to be the gnome? What the fuck is wrong with you?" White Shorts says.

"That bus is heading toward this street," the twenty-something watching the Sky Fox live feed says.

"Oh my god, I wish I could get a shot of it head on," White Shorts says. "Oh my god, could you get that shot for me?" she asks the bleeding police officer, who smiles and stands out in the roadway as the possessed shuttle bus flies around the corner and onto their block.

"Which button do I press?" the police officer asks before he is run over.

"My phone!" White Shorts says.

Chapter Six

A Brief Reflection on the Game of Centipede

Centipede was the very first video game to ever be created by a woman. Jimmy did not know this as a child, rolling the track ball at the arcade or playing on his Atari 2600 at home, but learning this knowledge later in life gave the game a special sort of allure, like it was a sacred snapshot into the female mind. The track ball, for one, was different from other games; in the arcade, you controlled the little gnome avatar at the bottom of the screen with a rolling track ball that guided the avatar back and forth as you shot upwards through rows of mushrooms and tried to hit the various body sections of the frantic centipede as it made its way down the screen through the garden forest. In the game, the avatar cannot run up to any point on the screen and begin attacking the centipede head-on—the avatar is relegated to the bottom of the screen, and Jimmy knows in the half-dead prodigy part of his mind that the attacks on the *Centipede*-controlled public transportation vehicles are failing because they aren't coming from the gnome avatar on the right place on the screen.

The fact that the avatar was supposed to be a gnome, or perhaps an elf, judging from the artwork on the Atari 2600 box, was ambiguous. As a child Jimmy imagined the avatar to be a little floating head that shot rays of light from its mouth, retaliating against the centipede for having such a full and superfluous body while the floating head had none, a body composed of round globes so excessive that destroying a segment merely split the creature into multiple violent parts that all continued to wind their way down to the bottom of the screen.

Jimmy had shared this idea with his father as a child, that the floating head avatar was fighting the centipede because it had a body and the head wanted a body, and his dad said the centipede is there so you can shoot it, that's it. But surely nothing created by a woman could be that simple, and as an adult it seemed increasingly obvious to Jimmy that the game was about destroying what you could not have. Jimmy feels shivers on his legs and a tightening in his stained gym shorts as he half-hardens at the beauty of this idea, and he sees the Korean women nod approvingly in his mind.

Chapter Seven

In Which Our Hero Steals an RPG

Jimmy runs toward the armored vehicles several blocks away to warn them that they're playing the game wrong. "You look so comfortable, so in control," the Russian woman says. Jimmy knows that at this point in the whisper video playing on the phone in his pocket, the cat has rolled onto its back and lets the Russian woman scrape her fingernails along the edges of its belly. Jimmy will often run his fingers along the sides of his own belly as he listens, but this is difficult to do while running, and he is also distracted by the repeating loops of social interaction replaying in his head: one playing back the interactions he had with White Shorts and the police officer and the other twentysomethings on the street corner, and one imaging the upcoming interaction he will need to have with the armored vehicles. He replays the eyes lingering on his sweat-stained Chuck E. Cheese work shirt. He is not sure how one speaks to an armored vehicle. Jimmy cannot even maintain a non-sexual erection given the circumstances. "You're very brave," the Russian woman whispers.

When Jimmy arrives at the armored vehicles, the vehicles begin shouting through incongruently low-quality speakers that he needs to leave the area. The Centipede shuttle bus is rapidly approaching this street. Up close, Jimmy sees that the vehicles are more like boxy, thick Hummers than tanks, and he runs up to one and pounds on the door. "Stop pounding on the door," a voice from the speaker says, but Jimmy does not stop and the door opens. Inside he can see three men, all dressed in black SWAT team uniforms and helmets. They have the Sky Fox news feed playing on an iPad resting against the gear shifter between the two front seats.

"It'll just keep sending more centipedes your way until you play the game right," Jimmy says. "It's playing a game of *Centipede* with you. You have to shoot it from the bottom of the screen. Here, I'll show you." Jimmy takes out his cell phone, which is still playing the Russian whisper video, and tries to search for a *Centipede* gameplay video by using Swype, but "centipede" keeps coming up as "gentle" or "centrifuge" and Jimmy isn't used to do doing too many searches or sending texts on his phone so he has a difficult time correcting the situation.

"Get the fuck out of here," one of the SWAT members says, and he grabs Jimmy's phone and the headphone jack comes out and now everyone is listening to the Russian whisper video still playing in the background while they also hear the lurching sounds of the Centipede bus approaching.

"I wish I could see inside your sweet, gentle thoughts," the Russian woman whispers. "What does cat dream of? I feel all tension falling from paws."

The SWAT team members are staring at Jimmy instead of at the bus heading directly for them and Jimmy can see that at least two of these men are younger than he is and all three are more attractive than he is and Jimmy might very well get run over by this rampaging Centipede bus in a few minutes and the Russian woman keeps talking and Jimmy thinks what the hell am I doing with my life. This is a thought that Jimmy has largely given up on, the thought that things could be different for him in his life, that he was perhaps not born to die standing in the doorway of an armored vehicle in a sweat-soaked Chuck E. Cheese shirt while the voice of a beautiful and kind Russian woman was being judged without defense. Jimmy wonders if it is the delirium of running for a sustained distance or the possibility of death by Atari monsters that makes him feel both like he is standing outside of himself and that he is hopelessly locked somewhere deep in his brain. He takes off his Chuck E.

Cheese shirt and stands before the SWAT team in a damp and moderately stained undershirt.

"So this is like a sex thing for you," the SWAT team member holding Jimmy's phone says.

The other two armored vehicles on scene have not been distracted by Jimmy's whisper video and emotionally significant undressing, and they have opened hatches on the tops of their cars and two uniformed men with rocket-propelled grenade launchers begin firing out of the hatches at the Centipede bus. The front windshield of the bus breaks out and some of the interior of the bus catches fire and the man who should have also fired on the bus but was instead nodding like it made sense that this would be a sex thing for Jimmy tries to get through the hatch on the roof of his armored vehicle as well.

The bus, badly damaged and in flames, collides with the front two armored vehicles, which jerks one of the shooters, and his rocket-propelled grenade launcher is thrown to the ground. Jimmy runs for it, grabs it, and though it weighs far more than he had anticipated, begins running with it over his shoulder toward the point on the screen where the shooting should have been coming from to begin with.

He is about three blocks away and still running when he realizes the SWAT team member still has his phone and that his phone is somewhere in the bus-Hummer collision and that he has now lost his whisper videos. Jimmy can see his phone resting in the lifeless and/or bleeding hand of the SWAT team member, the Russian woman still massaging her cat and narrating the experience to no one, like she must have done when she recorded the video. Even though he could only half listen to the video before, the fact that those voices existed, pressed against his thigh, inside of his phone, waiting for him, had been a comfort, and he imagines that it was always a kind of comfort for the whispering women too.

Without it, he feels his legs dissolving under the weight of the RPG slung over his shoulder; first his calves are gone after half a block, then his knees rub away as they nub him onward, then his body flops face down on the sidewalk, pulsing forward with awkward baby-crawling spurts as the skin on his face is torn away by sidewalk pebbles. But his legs have not dissolved, and they keep running forward, and there is a sharp but manageable cramp in Jimmy's side, and he can feel sweat dripping down the backs of his thighs, and it all reminds him that the world still exists despite the loss of his cell phone and the introduction of the Atari game invasion.

Jimmy tries to imagine a conversation with the Korean women to distract himself from the great loss of his whisper videos and asks them whether they think there is a connection between understanding women and understanding the mechanics of the female-created *Centipede* game, and the Korean women just giggle and shrug because they really don't know a thing about *Centipede* or what he's talking about. Jimmy considers that the brief interaction with White Shorts earlier was the most extensive female interaction he has had in a very long time so he feels pretty open to any and all insights at this point in his life, *Centipede*-based or not. He wonders whether his inclination to read this much into an 8-bit video game might, in fact, be part of the problem.

He is beginning to explain the game to the Korean women in his mind when he sees that up ahead there is a two-car accident in the road and a few people standing around and one person screaming and running past Jimmy in the opposite direction. There is a woman lying down on the sidewalk who is not injured, staring at a bloody unmoving man stretched across the center of the street and she is wearing a blue dress with tiny yellow flowers and she is not moving. She is making an ooo ooo ooo sound like the saddest cow that has ever lived and some people are taking pictures and Jimmy has to jump over her body to keep running and his stomach clenches to keep from vomiting and the Korean women disappear and he wishes that he had his whisper videos again.

Chapter Eight

In Which Our Hero Joins the Gun Pride Thursday Militia

Jimmy turns onto a street that he believes is far enough down to begin properly shooting from the position of the gnome avatar and immediately runs into a group of thirty some odd men, all armed, wearing Wrangler jeans and cowboy hats. The cowboy hats are just worn enough that they show signs of Real Cowboy Wear but not so worn as to be excluded from possibly being part of a Visit to the City outfit, a look that Jimmy recognizes from a certain population of parents who inexplicably find themselves attending a children's birthday party at a Chuck E. Cheese in downtown Denver. Some of the men are half-heartedly holding signs that read "Don't Tread on Me" and "Know Guns, Know Peace."

"Hey, Glen," one of the armed cowboys yells, "is this your nephew? Whoa there, fella," the cowboy says, catching Jimmy by the shoulder as Jimmy attempts to run past the group to get a shot between the buildings at the winding Centipede bus.

"Shoot, that ain't my nephew," Glen says, walking over and tipping his hat at Jimmy. "Cody always says he'll come but he never does. I wish that boy would take things more seriously. It's his freedom we're fighting for."

"I really need to start shooting at this Centipede bus," Jimmy says, unsuccessfully trying to pull away from the cowboy holding his shoulder.

"Now hold up, boy. Wait here a minute. What you doing coming out here all sweaty with a grenade launcher if you're not joining up for Gun Pride Thursday? What's going on?"

Jimmy explains, as briefly as he can, that the city is under attack by a giant Atari game cartridge that has taken over public transportation and turned it into a live version of *Centipede*.

"God damn it, so this is how it starts," the old cowboy says, letting go of Jimmy's shoulder. "It's real, boys," he yells to the crowd. "This is it." Then he turns back to Jimmy. "We march once a month on the capital for Gun Pride Thursdays. We meet up a few blocks from here, at Walter's house"—a man toward the back of the crowd waves at Jimmy, indicating that he is Walter—"and shoot if we weren't confused about all the commotion and explosions going on as we were heading this-a-way. But here it is," he says, pulling a large, long-barreled hand gun out of the holster on his hip. "They're coming for our guns."

"It's a giant Atari game," Jimmy says.

"God damn right. Classic liberal diversion tactics. Oh, it's an alien. Oh, it's giant Nintendo Godzilla. Nope. It's your own God damn government." And the old cowboy spits, and the other cowboys drop their signs and pull out their guns if they weren't already out, and all these men are looking at Jimmy, and Jimmy realizes that they are waiting for him to lead them, that he is now the leader of a heavily armed Colorado gun advocacy militia. The closest thing to a gun that Jimmy has ever fired is the red plastic *House of the Dead* gun at the Chuck E. Cheese arcade, and even then he wasn't very good at it. He was too distracted by the boxy woman in the red sweater getting eaten slowly by boxy zombies to fire on the demon frogs leaping toward him and he wondered if he could maybe play the game as one of the zombies instead and have a conversation with the boxy red sweater woman before apologetically eating her.

Jimmy feels vomit rise up in his throat and he thinks of the Russian woman massaging her cat and he swallows his vomit and hears the Russian woman repeating that Jimmy is very brave. "We need to spread out along this block and fire up between the buildings at the bus that's winding through," Jimmy says, his voice shaking. The men nod and start to fan out without question, setting themselves up along alleyways that have clear shots through several blocks. Jimmy wonders how they accepted him so quickly and is glad that he is no longer wearing his rodent pants or his Chuck E. Cheese shirt, and then he also remembers his rocket-propelled grenade launcher, which must add some kind of masculine authority to his doughy, pale figure.

He jogs up to where the old cowboy has positioned himself, and the old cowboy says, "Well shit, son, get ready if you want to fire that thing off," and Jimmy realizes that he has no idea how to fire an RPG and he holds the weapon in both hands and stares at it.

"Give the God damn thing to me," Glen, whose nephew never comes to the gun parade with him, says, and the old cowboys smacks Glen's reaching hands away from Jimmy's weapon. "He'll never learn if you don't take the time to let him try, Glen. Why do you think your nephew doesn't want to spend any time with you? Shit." And the old cowboy lifts the RPG up on Jimmy's shoulder, places Jimmy's hand on the trigger, and yells "GO!" when they see the bus appear two streets over and Jimmy fires and the rest of the men begin firing and someone screams like they've been clipped by a bullet and some windows from the businesses facing the shooters get hit and shatter glass onto the street and the bus centipede is hit multiple times and stops moving altogether.

Jimmy is about to tell the cowboys where they need to go to shoot the other two Centipede light rail trains when a black armored Hummer like the ones that had been shooting from the wrong location a few blocks away pulls up and throws open a back door. "Get in," a man wearing a black suit and sunglasses says to Jimmy.

Chapter Nine

An Old Foe Wagers on the End of the World

In a windowless poker lounge in Reno, Nevada, Jimmy's father drains the last bit of his Budweiser and glances up at the muted television above the bar. He can't read the ticker feed at the bottom of the screen, but he can see that a giant black block is shooting out lasers and killing people in downtown Denver and that deranged light rail cars are running people over in the streets. The aerial footage shows Jimmy and the gang of cowboys firing on the Centipede bus but Jimmy's father wouldn't be able to recognize Jimmy even if the shot had been a close up on his face and included the caption "JIMMY TOLEDO, FORMER ARCADE CHAMP, BATTLES MONSTER BUS."

Jimmy's father gestures to the television and asks the bartender if this is some kind of apocalypse and the bartender shrugs and Jimmy's father asks if he can put $50 on the end of the world. The news feed cuts to a dump in New Mexico with a giant chasm in it where the massive Atari cartridge arose from the dirt and small chunks of the Atari E.T. game are flopping around in the irradiated soil like dying fish. The bartender unmutes the TV and the reporter says that the E.T. games left at the site are not believed to be a threat because of their impossibly boring and nonviolent content. The megacartridge that flew into Denver, however, is believed to be motivated by the competitive, aggressive nature of the games that fed into it as it baked into a horrible mutant monster in the radioactive earth over the past three decades. The bartender turns the sound off again and says it doesn't look like the apocalypse, just some monster shooting up Denver, and Jimmy's father sighs and says that figures.

The mention of the Atari games makes him think of the old arcade circuit, and he briefly considers mentioning to the bartender that he used to be a champion player back in the day, as this is something he tells people from time to time and occasionally believes. He never mentions Jimmy when he brings this up to people because Jimmy is just one in a failed string of children and relationships, something stored in the same category of his mind as attempting to change his own car oil in the driveway and ruining a good pair of pants in the process. But the bartender is taking another order and Jimmy's father doesn't feel that continuing the conversation would be a net gain for him in the end, so he shuts off the fountain of fabricated memories and digs in his pocket for beer money. Even though some part of him knows that Jimmy is likely still in the Denver area, he doesn't really think of that as he turns away from the television and the bar, fresh Budweiser in hand, preferring to sleepwalk through his memories the same way he likes to sleepwalk through life, not remembering any of the details of his morning drive to this dive bar, just somehow always arriving in the same place every day.

Chapter Ten

In Which Our Hero is Recruited by the Government

Jimmy is sitting at a particle board table across from two men in black suits in a 1970s metal trailer with worn orange carpeting located in a park at the base of the Colorado capital building, just a few blocks from the 16th Street Mall and the epicenter of the Atari invasion. There is a banner hanging on the wall behind the two men in the black suits that reads HELENA CONSTRUCTION AND SEWAGE SOLUTIONS and there are bent, rolled up blueprints and files piled on the ground as if they had been hastily swept off the table as part of a last minute government acquisition of this metal trailer turned operations hub. The thin door of the trailer opens and a skinny man in a white collared shirt with the sleeves rolled up walks in with computer equipment and takes it into the only other room in the trailer, shutting the door behind him. Jimmy knows that these men are with the government because they told him that when they dragged him into their Hummer away from the militia men. Now Jimmy is staring at the fake wood finish on the particle board table and repeating a song in his head about how to start conversations with people when you become very nervous at the thought of starting a conversation with new people: When you meet a new person/you should ask for their name/ then they'll ask you the same/then you'll ask why they came/ to the place where you hang/You can ask what they do/if they know so-and-so too/what do they think of the food.

"Jimmy," the older man in the suit says, "we need your help."

"Okay," Jimmy says. The old man has a head that is square on the bottom but round and bald on the top, like R2-

D2, Jimmy thinks, except with more nose hair and forehead furrows.

"We're willing to make this profitable for you," R2-D2 says.

"Okay," Jimmy says. One word answers/are never the way/to make someone remember/what you have to say.

"I think he said okay to helping us without the profitable part, sir," the younger man in the suit says.

"Who are you working for, Jimmy?" R2-D2 asks.

"Chuck E. Cheese," Jimmy says.

"Don't fuck with us," the older man says.

"Okay," Jimmy says. You never know where/a simple how-do-you-do/will end up leading you, Jimmy sings in his head. He does not want to be singing this in his head as he does not want to be meeting these men but he can't stop the looping image of cartoon people gathering at a cartoon party and singing this mediocre advice song, a video Jimmy had found once online when Googling different strategies for talking to people, strategies he could not evaluate as he had never tried them, but this song has melted into his head and resurfaces occasionally on repeat at inappropriate times.

"We know everything about you, Jimmy," R2-D2 says. "We know about your champion arcade days. We know you know everything about these games. How they work. How they think."

"You know what they want, Jimmy," the younger man in the suit says. "What do they want?"

"Um," Jimmy says.

"That's not a rhetorical question, Jimmy," R2-D2 says. "We have a recording of you talking with our SWAT team, telling them how to beat these things. We saw the Sky Fox footage of you helping those crazies you're with blow up that bus. Thornton, pull up that footage." The younger man pulls out an iPhone and starts tapping at the screen.

"It was loading earlier," Thornton, the younger man, says.

"We just watched that. It should be right there. Refresh—refresh the thing," R2-D2 says. Thornton taps the screen

37

again and waits. R2-D2 reaches across him and jabs at the screen.

"Now you just closed it," Thornton says.

"Ricky," R2-D2 shouts. "Ricky!" The thin man who had brought in the computer equipment opens the door and Jimmy can see a few computers getting set up on similar particle board tables in the other room. "Can you come out here and get this thing to go?"

"I know I was there!" Jimmy says, and the two men in the suits look up from the phone, and Ricky, approaching slowly from the doorway, stops awkwardly in mid-gangly-stride. "It's fine. I'll help you. I'm not working for the cowboys and I know I was helping them and I don't need to watch the video and I would like to help you." The cartoon party people from the YouTube song playing in Jimmy's head stop singing and stare at him.

"So what does it want, Jimmy?" R2-D2 asks. "What does it want? The game?"

"I don't know," Jimmy says. "I was just guessing that it wanted to be played."

Chapter Eleven

An Uneasy Alliance is Formed

Jimmy is riding in a Hummer with the suit men to a rendezvous point where the protesting cowboys and the uninjured SWAT team members are waiting. Jimmy confirmed his theory with the suit men before leaving the trailer—they watched on the Sky Fox news feed as the Centipede bus, stopped by cowboy firepower, burned in the street. The Atari game's glowing *Centipede* logo flickered in the helicopter's aerial shot of downtown Denver but remained lit, and the cartridge didn't send out an animating bolt of electricity to force another bus or light rail car to take the fallen Centipede bus's place. Seeing that he was correct, that playing the game might be a way to defeat this monster, gave Jimmy a warm tingling burst that ran from the back of his neck to the span of his shoulders, down his spine, and into his groin, a feeling of satisfaction that rivaled the feeling he had when he watched his first whisper video: a close-up on a smiling woman's face, her moist lips parting slowly as she said how good it was to see you.

There are still two more light rail trains prowling the city blocks, however, and the suit men got their SWAT team contacts to recruit the Gun Pride Thursday cowboys to split up into two teams to take them on. Other help was coming—forces are flying in, R2-D2 says, with troops from Peterson Air Force Base in Colorado Springs expected to arrive first, but the cowboys are eager and, according to the suit men, expendable.

They pull up to the site and a group of cowboys and SWAT team members are waiting. "If we all had our own God damn tanks—our Constitutional right to have our own

God damn tanks—none of this would be happening," the old cowboy is saying to no one in particular. He nods to Jimmy. "Somebody give this boy a gun," he says, and one of the younger cowboys hands Jimmy some kind of assault rifle that Jimmy has no idea how to fire, like the kind mounted on the *Terminator 2: Judgment Day* cabinet at the Chuck E. Cheese arcade, except without the orange tip, and Jimmy decides that he will just try squeezing the trigger once the Centipede train comes and hope that no one will notice if nothing happens. The assault rifle is heavy and he isn't sure how to hold it or what to do with his hands while he waits with everyone, and he feels a bit like when he's in the rat suit at work and it's not quite time for the birthday party to start so maybe there's two or three kids there, and their parents, and Jimmy is standing off to the side of the party table unable to really talk through his rat head and the children are obviously just tolerating this as a means to acquire cake and the mothers are trying to see Jimmy through the near-opaque mesh eyes, thinking Jimmy is probably a pedophile.

They hear the light rail before they can see it between the buildings. "Is that it?" R2-D2 asks, and Thornton, the younger suit man, checks his live Sky Fox video stream on his phone and says, "Yeah, that looks like a light rail train a few blocks up," and the SWAT team members get into position and the cowboys get into position and Jimmy holds the gun up so the butt is pressed against his right shoulder and he worries that the gun will kick and hurt his shoulder because he cries easily.

The light rail car is now two blocks up and the group can see it flashing between the city buildings and alleyways as it races forward and everyone begins to fire and Jimmy pulls the trigger and his gun fires a stream of bullets and slams into Jimmy's shoulder and Jimmy's arm jerks up and he shoots out some of the glass on the building to the right of the alleyway he was shooting down but no one seems to notice. Jimmy stops firing but holds his gun in position as if he is firing and he feels like he is getting away with not really learning his recorder part for the second grade pageant all over again, with both that feeling of small success that comes when your failures go unnoticed and that confused, stomach-drop feeling that wishes someone had been there to notice.

This train is several cars long. The SWAT team at one end of the street have stopped two of the cars dead and the cowboys a third and Jimmy none. The remaining two cars round the next block and race ahead, now just one street away from the shooters, and Jimmy half-squeezes the trigger on his gun, not hard enough to fire, and remembers his little boy fingers as they skimmed along the smooth track ball orb of a *Centipede* arcade game controller, and instead of the eyes of his father or the eyes of no one he feels the smiling eyes of his twin Korean women in their starched white lab coats and he can almost hear them speaking beautiful psychic thoughts to each other about him.

And the gun fire stops and Jimmy looks up and the light rail train is dead one block up from them and some of the cowboys start singing "America the Beautiful" and Jimmy turns to see that over his shoulder the suit men have been watching the Sky Fox live feed this whole time instead of watching the actual destruction of possessed public transportation happening right in front of them. The other team of cowboys and SWAT members has been attacking the third and final Centipede light rail train to the north of the 16th Street Mall and the younger suit man says, "What the hell is happening with the game?" and Jimmy jogs over to them to watch the feed on the younger suit man's cell phone and tells the Korean women in his mind to stop singing along with the cowboys in their imaginary whisper-quiet accented English.

On the screen Jimmy and the suit men see all three centipedes dead and smoldering—the bus that was destroyed first, the light rail train one block in front of them, and the third light rail train burning blocks away. The *Centipede* game logo on the huge black video game cartridge is flashing like it's losing power, then it goes completely black and remains black long enough for some people to cautiously exit the office building lobbies and bars near the Atari game in order to take more pictures. After a few minutes of relative peace the cartridge again shoots out huge white streams of lightning and the people who aren't struck scatter and the front of the game blinks and bursts into a full glow like what happens after the final bulb in a sketchy Christmas tree light string gets replaced, and the cartridge burns bright with the *Frogger* logo.

"What the fuck does that mean?" R2-D2 asks, and before Jimmy can answer the Atari cartridge is shooting out beams of energy and animating all the cars parked along the city streets in three huge rings around the 16th Street Mall.

Chapter Twelve

The People of Denver Demonstrate Their Need for a Hero

The suits and Jimmy watch on the younger suit's cell phone as the Sky Fox live stream shrinks into a small box on the upper left-hand corner of the screen and the broad grinning face of a junior field reporter, Trevor "Feet on the Ground" Abana, appears. Abana is sitting awkwardly on a bar stool at This Must Be the Place, a bar on the 16th Street Mall wedged between office buildings and cluttered with thrift store board games, vintage books, and other pieces of forced personality that remain untouched by patrons because the only people that frequent the bar are tourists dragging their feet on their way to the mountains or business people working entry-level downtown jobs who are eager to let kitsch fill the blank spot where their own personality might otherwise go. Abana describes the bar's patrons as refugees of the Game Over: Denver crisis, the official Fox name for the Atari situation, and as the camera does a slow pan around the small, intentionally dark space the 20- and 30-somethings in off-the-rack business wear lift their pints of Shock Top Belgium-style Anheuser-Busch and self-consciously applaud their own hardship.

"Yeah, we've been here since like the thing plugged in," a young man being interviewed by Abana says. "Our building lost power pretty quick after that thing crashed so we were like, hey, can we go? And our boss was like, 'Whatever, just don't get zapped by that thing on the clock.' Which is hilarious because it's not like I'm hourly or anything," and the young man laughs and a young woman sitting next to him smacks him on the shoulder in way orchestrated to provide a lingering touch while she feigns outrage.

"Well I am hourly," the young woman says. "We work on the same floor but I'm a social media intern and I'm still working," and she shakes an iPhone held in her non-shoulder-lingering hand. "Actually this has been pretty awesome because we've gotten so many more followers for Timble and Timble LLC because of this. And when Molly died—Molly's our intern coordinator—holy crap you should have seen the reply tweet spike. Just feeling really fortunate right now that all this goes so well with our branding."

The reporter turns away abruptly from the pair and says, "But that's not the real story from the epicenter of Game Over: Denver," and as the camera follows Abana off of his bar stool it catches a glimpse of the young woman looking let down that she is not the real story and the young man next to her positions himself to turn her disappointed face into an uninspired but adequate sexual encounter.

The camera refocuses as it gets a crooked shot out the bar's front window toward a street where the Atari cartridge has animated a number of cars and trucks, forcing them to drive at varying speeds in a perimeter around the 16th Street Mall area where the Atari game is lodged into the ground. There is a crowd of people on both sides of the street and one person jumps out into the street and is immediately run over by a white Ford pickup truck with no driver. There is a glare on the bar's front window and the shot is terrible anyhow and Abana asks to go to the Sky Fox shot and the small Sky Fox box expands out and takes over the whole screen again.

"So you can see here—if we could zoom out a little more—perfect—so you can see here how we've got these three rings of traffic circling our ground zero site here,"—and Abana superimposes red hand-drawn lines over the pathway of the self-driving vehicles, as though it were a sports replay and the viewer could somehow not see the aerial shot of the cars driving, some slow, some fast, in concentric squares around the 16th Street Mall.

"And I think we've got that death counter ready to go up," Abana says, and a small graphic appears in the lower-right hand corner of the screen that reads "DEATH COUNT:

500." "Well, that number can't be right, can it? I mean I don't think 500 people have died down here yet. And that's such an even number, Steve. It doesn't even look real. Can you confirm that or fix that? Steve?" But the 500 number stays on the screen and the man who was run over by the white pickup truck has now also been hit by a blue Camry and a black Geo Metro and Steve has either dropped the ball on the Death Counter graphic or just doesn't give a fuck about Abana's segment, and Jimmy, still watching with the suits at the site of the fallen Centipede light rail train, wonders if defeating *Frogger* will be any easier than *Centipede* because he's pretty sure someone's going to have jump across the tops of some of those speeding cars.

Chapter Thirteen

In Which Our Hero Becomes a Doctor

"You're going on in ten," R2-D2 says. R2-D2 and Jimmy are back in the Hummer.

"Going on where?" Jimmy asks.

"On air, Bobby. You're doing a press conference."

"What?" Jimmy asks.

"You're going to answer some questions about what's going on," R2-D2 says. "We need to tell the people something and God knows I can't be seen on the air."

"Why not?" Jimmy asks.

"For Christ's sake, can you see what I look like? You think I choose to look like a no-neck trash can?" R2-D2 asks. "You and Riles here are going to put a face on this situation." R2-D2 points to the large man in the front seat of the Hummer, wearing padded black tactical armor that Jimmy expects might include an embroidered white and red Umbrella Corporation logo but does not and Riles turns around to smile at Jimmy and he has large white Tom Cruise teeth and no eyes, only mirrored aviators that reflect back two pale, sweaty, captive Jimmies.

"Just answer some questions and tell people to stay inside," R2-D2 continues, and Riles is still turned around and looking at Jimmy with his teeth. "You don't know any compromising information, Jackie, but if you do manage to say something compromising, we'll just push you in front of the Nintendo and let it zap your balls off and I'll call up my goddamn grandson and get him to tell me how to beat this fucking Pong machine." Riles sucks air in what could be mistaken for a laugh but Jimmy knows Riles is tasting the air for the scent of his own superiority.

46

Jimmy is a little frightened and his feelings are hurt but he knows that R2-D2 is only trying to motivate him to do well at this press conference and that R2-D2 does value Jimmy's service even if he can't remember Jimmy's name and he wouldn't have brought Jimmy here if he didn't believe in him. It was like Jimmy's father used to say before tournaments: I wouldn't have brought you here if I thought you were going to be terrible and make a goddamn fool out of me. It makes Jimmy want to do right by R2-D2 the same way he wanted to do right by his father, which gives Jimmy a tingling in his stomach in the tingling range just below the sexual but above the nauseous fearful, the kind of suspended breath-holding feeling he gets if he sees a stray dog and he's reaching out his hand to touch it but he's concerned that it might bite him because what if someone saw the poor thing bite him and then called animal control and animal control chopped the dog's head off to check for rabies all because of Jimmy?

The Hummer arrives at the local Fox station's building, about two miles away from the 16th Street Mall, and Jimmy and R2-D2 and Riles get out of the car while the driver stays in the car with the engine running, and Jimmy wonders if the driver will turn the radio on and listen to music or if he has something with him to read or if the driver is just supposed to sit there because he's working and he's compelled to do his duty and be a team player in a way that Jimmy is beginning to struggle with. Jimmy and R2-D2 and Riles are led into the building by a chubby brunette woman with her hair up in a messy bun that conveys both order and stress, and one of her small, carefully manicured hands is gripping a clipboard so tight that the pads on her fingers are glowing white where the wood of the board digs into her flesh. Jimmy forgets the intimidating teeth of Riles and feels himself start to grow hard looking at this woman's small, round, pressurized fingertips, the kind of fingers that could be stars in the soothing sounds online video community. In his mind Jimmy pictures this chubby, vaguely hostile brunette as the star of a YouTube channel based entirely around wooden sounds, the tapping of chopsticks against a wooden table, the sound of large bark chips rolled quickly and then slowly between her plush palms, all this done without talking, maybe even without a face shot. He imagines her fingers running along a yellow number two pencil's hexagonal planes, a shot of her pressing hard into the pencil, before finally snapping it in two.

Jimmy is brought into a green screen room that says WEATHER CENTER in abrasive, threatening lettering and he is sat in a chair next to Riles and told to look straight ahead and Riles is told to look straight ahead and Riles refuses to take off this sunglasses. In front of Jimmy is a camera and a cameraman and a teleprompter and in front of Riles is a separate camera and cameraman and teleprompter. Between the sets of cameras is a television monitor with several different split screens on it, one showing the Sky Fox live stream of the Atari cartridge carnage, one showing a silent view of Colorado's governor reading a statement from his office, and one showing a team of national Fox anchors staring straight at Jimmy as if they can already see him directly through the screen sitting here with an erection that is half fear and half arousal. Chubby Pressure Fingers comes over to Jimmy and clips a small black mic on the stretched neck hole of his stained white undershirt and she can clearly see Jimmy's erection straining against the mesh material of his Chuck E. Cheese communal under-rat-suit gym shorts. Jimmy knows that she can see it and he isn't sure if he should apologize or pretend he doesn't have an erection and he can feel the sweat growing again under his armpits and around his ball sack and decides to pretend that he doesn't have an erection. He closes his eyes as Chubby's stray brunette hairs brush past his jaw and neck and he can smell her and she smells very ordinary and clean, like maybe she doesn't care about brand names and exotic floral oils and just uses the generic King Soopers shampoo, which Jimmy finds admirable.

Jimmy watches Chubby bend over to clip a mic onto Riles and Riles sits with his teeth exposed, mouth breathing, like a snake that draws all information from the air. Jimmy is

48

somewhat envious of this ability, to understand the situation and your place in it from the physical properties of smells within a five foot radius, but figures that being able to think in words is probably more advantageous, even when those words get stuck in grating razorblade loops of repetition in your head.

A man in the doorway who looks like he works at the station tells Jimmy that he has thirty seconds until he is live and Jimmy asks, "How does this work?" because he both isn't sure what he's supposed to say and he also doesn't think that this looks like a press conference because the only image he has of a press conference is when politicians admit that they're gay or tweeting pictures of their dicks and they stand in front of a podium and they sometimes have their very awful looking wives and families next to them. Jimmy wants to ask why they are in the WEATHER CENTER and the man in the doorway shakes his head quickly like he can read Jimmy's mind and Jimmy is definitely not in the WEATHER CENTER and then the two camera men hold up three, two, one fingers and suddenly Jimmy can see his own face on the monitor in front of him with a fake computer lab type background behind his head and Riles' face is in a separate split screen box with the Atari cartridge rising up dramatically behind his head as though he is out on the street in the line of fire. A small box still remains for the aerial Sky Fox shot of the *Frogger*-possessed cars and the national Fox anchors' faces suddenly contort and animate like they, too, are being controlled by the monster cartridge.

"We're live now with Dr. James Turlington, a government operative whose unparalleled knowledge of this gaming nightmare has saved countless lives so far," a thin, middle-aged blonde woman with feathered hair says at Jimmy through the TV, and Jimmy's first reaction is to start shaking his head slowly because that's not his name and her description is similarly misguided but Jimmy stops himself mid-shake because he does not want to be replaced by R2-D2's grandson yet.

"It's to be here," Jimmy says, raising one hand stoically, not sure if he really just said, "it's to be here," out loud rather than "it's great to be here" or if he just thinks that he omitted the "great" from his greeting and while he replays his comment in his head he leaves his hand hanging in the air like a child with a question. His erection has not gone away and while the feather-haired woman introduces Riles, Jimmy tries to flex his thigh muscles because he read that flexing your thigh muscles diverts the blood flow away from an unwelcomed erection, but it only causes Jimmy to squirm-bounce a little in his seat with his child's hand still raised as Riles fake-describes the ground conditions that he's pretending to be in.

"What I want to know is this, Dr. Turlington," an overweight reporter in a brown suit sitting next to Feathered Hair says to Jimmy, who does not immediately remember that he is supposed to be Dr. Turlington. "How does our government manage to keep a video game expert on their payroll the other 364 days of the year when we're not being attacked by a giant flying waste of time and how is it that the government says they know for sure this thing crawled up out of U.S. soil and isn't a direct threat from the Empire of Japan?" Riles doesn't say anything and Jimmy doesn't say anything and a flood of fear washes across Jimmy's stomach and he stops flexing his thighs and remembers that maybe he is supposed to answer Dr. Turlington-related questions. He notices that the teleprompter has been running this whole time with canned responses to give to Feathered Hair and Brown Suit but the first part of his response is cut off because the text is scrolling fast like a *Tetris* screen that is stacking up past the point of repair and Jimmy sees himself getting shot in point-blank range by Riles or worse: getting dropped back off at Chuck E. Cheese with a new empty rat suit waiting.

Riles steps in and says that it's not Dr. Turlington's place to answer questions like this and it's really a waste of his time to stand for this level of harassment and do the Fox anchors actually want more people to die because this doctor government operative expert was getting interrogated over budget questions? And Jimmy is relieved and looks over to Riles in silent thanks, which looks odd on the monitor because Riles and Jimmy are in front of different green screen images and are not really supposed to be sitting next to each other in the Denver Fox station WEATHER CENTER.

As Riles continues talking and Jimmy considers that Riles is perhaps not so bad a guy, Jimmy notices that his teleprompter is filling with text so he can answer a question that has not yet been asked and before Jimmy can really start reading the text Feathered Hair asks, "What can you tell us about your strategy moving forward with this second phase of the invasion?" And Jimmy takes a deep breath and thinks I'm on national television and my boss could be watching and the Korean women could be watching and maybe even somewhere out there my dad could be watching, and while Jimmy is thinking this the teleprompter text has already begun to move and Jimmy knows he will have to abandon his cocoon of thoughts and answer the question himself.

"It's...*Frogger*," Jimmy says quietly, trying not to stammer, pushing away the stabbing thoughts that repeat over and over that he is wearing a disgusting stained undershirt and has greasy, matted hair and that there are elementary school-aged children who have higher *Frogger* scores than he currently does at Chuck E. Cheese. "So. *Frogger*. The Atari cartridge wants you to play whatever game it's trying to act out. So for this one, you would run between cars in the outer-most perimeter of traffic, and then probably jump from the tops of the cars in the inner two perimeters of the traffic," Jimmy says, beginning to squeeze his thigh muscles again, rummaging through cycles of repetitive thoughts for something comforting to fixate on but unable to focus on anything except the sound of his own slow and slightly nasal voice. "So someone would start from the outside loop and work their way in toward the cartridge in the center to defeat it. Well, five someones, probably, because I think it wants to clear the level. And each level you get five little frogs that you've got to get into their little homes on the other side of the river." Feathered Hair stares at Jimmy blankly and Jimmy wonders if she is staring because what he was supposed to read off the teleprompter was different from what he actually said or if she was staring because he is clearly a terrible choice to serve as a fake doctor government operative expert.

"Really," Jimmy adds, jiggling up and down slightly in his seat as he pulses his thigh muscles, "anybody could give this a shot. You'd just have to be good at running and jumping. I guess you could die..." And Jimmy shrugs, because people are already eager to die, it seems, so they might as well die trying to defeat this *Frogger* stage and see what happens next.

Feathered Hair asks Riles about the special military forces arriving in Denver to help control the situation and Jimmy can see on the Sky Fox aerial feed on the monitor in front of him that more people are now starting to gather around the Atari-controlled Frogger vehicles and it isn't long before a flood of them race across the street, tripping over each other, falling underneath the wheels of unyielding traffic. Jimmy thinks that most of them look happy, at least from this removed aerial shot. R2-D2 appears in the doorway and motions for Jimmy to get up and come over to him. Jimmy mouths, "Now?" and gets up carefully from his seat and hopes that his erection has subsided enough to not be noticeable as he stands up but it has not subsided enough and R2-D2 does not look pleased with Jimmy, though Jimmy does not think it has to do with his erection.

Chapter Fourteen

In Which Frogger Inspires Reflections Upon Mortality

After justifying their daytime drinking and bar bathroom blowjobs with spirited conversations about the apocalypse and how this was their last chance ever to catch guilt-free strange, the bored office workers and out of town visitors stranded in the many tacky, overpriced bars along the 16th Street Mall were encouraged by Jimmy's message that anyone could be a hero if they could just run and jump with some level of proficiency. Men struggling through their refractory period and men frustrated that they couldn't even get a handjob on what was likely their last day on earth, along with women looking for the ultimate one-up story about how they casually helped save the world this one time, came stumbling out of the bars, eager to give this running and jumping across traffic thing a try.

Jimmy is standing at the outmost ring of Frogger traffic with R2-D2 and Riles and some other military operatives who have arrived from Colorado Springs, watching as the cars speed bump over dozens of dead bodies in the road. "At least it slows the cars down, I'll give you that," R2-D2 says, though Jimmy knows that he is still disappointed that Jimmy didn't stick to his script and has made cleanup more complicated.

Jimmy looks at the bodies and his eyes linger on an intact young woman's face, eyes closed, neck flattened and torn open, white collared work shirt soaked with blood and twisted legs still wearing business appropriate black heels. Jimmy knows that this woman would not have been the first person to attempt to cross this ring of traffic, that she could have just as easily stayed in whatever safe hiding spot she'd been in up to this point, but instead must have stepped out into the road in her high heels just for something to do. He does not feel guilty about her death, but instead sees this woman walking into the stream of cars, perhaps laughing as she runs forward with some uncertainty in her heels in an incredible moment of bravery and beauty in a world otherwise stitched shut in its ordinary, repetitive ugliness.

The men's bodies, however, do not inspire the same sort of response from Jimmy, and in their broken jaws and exposed brain matter he sees mostly yelling, taunting, fear, and a motivation to run into traffic in order to live up to someone's idea of being strong. He wonders why he ran outside in his rat suit when he could have stayed in Chuck E. Cheese, if he was afraid of how embarrassing it would be in someone else's eyes—his father's eyes?—to die in a rat suit while children threw pepperoni at him and called him gay. He hopes that walking out was a choice he made for himself, a choice to try and be a different person one last time, instead of being one more reaction of fear oozing out of the past.

Jimmy pats his pants pockets instinctively for his phone, which he knows is gone, and imagines slipping earbuds into his ears and starting up a whisper video on creative organizational ideas for the home or a step-by-step guide to folding paper cranes. He feels the shaky, sick feeling that often accompanies his moments of self-reflection and evaluation, the feeling that he'd rather rip out each one of his fingernails than spend any more time alone with himself inside of his head.

Riles tells Jimmy that he's ready to lead the first non-civilian group through the Frogger traffic rings and Jimmy is thankful for the forced reprieve from his own thoughts. Jimmy explains to Riles and four other huge men similarly dressed in padded tactical gear that they need to watch for the patterns in the movement of the traffic in order to make it through successfully and that he's not entirely sure if this will work or what will happen when all five of them get to the cartridge at the center of the three rings of traffic. Riles' team members are all wearing ear pieces and Jimmy has a walkie-talkie in one hand and a live feed of the Sky Fox aerial coverage on R2-D2's iPad in his other hand, which Jimmy is supposed to use to guide the team through the layers of traffic. Jimmy is not exactly sure how he will do this but he said he would be willing to try, namely because not trying was not an option. Some other SWAT team members tried to clear the area of civilians, but there is still a crowd of drunk, bored observers calling out as if this were a sporting event or a very engaging television show. Some people are still trying to run into traffic, but there is too much road to cover to really put up a protective barrier, and crunches and splats in the distance are typically followed up by cheering or, more rarely, screaming.

As Riles and his team step into traffic Jimmy imagines how a whisper artist might narrate their journey toward the center Atari cartridge. "If you move quickly now, you have time to slow down later," he imagines his favorite Russian-accented YouTube video star saying. "Left, left, right. Pause for a moment, one, two. That's it. You're doing so well. I'm so proud of you for trying."

"We're across the first street," Riles says through the walkie-talkie, which is not really necessary to say because Jimmy can clearly see him across the street and Riles can probably see Jimmy as well because Jimmy can see himself reflected between passing cars in Riles' mirrored aviators. "Also what the fuck were you talking about back there?" Riles adds through the walkie-talkie, and Jimmy wonders if he actually said any of what he was thinking out loud. Riles and his team start jogging up the block toward the next street that they will need to cross, this time crossing on the tops of the cars like the cars are a pathway across a river. In the Sky Fox feed Jimmy can see some of the Gun Pride Thursday cowboy militia marchers hanging around the edge of the street and a few fallen cowboy hats getting trampled over and over again by the vehicles that are standing in for *Frogger*'s floating logs and unstable turtles, and Jimmy is glad to see that the cowboys have made it this far and that they are still armed and still carrying their protest signs.

Riles and his team are dragging tables and boxes out of nearby restaurants and bars to use as platforms off of which to jump on top of the cars, and Jimmy glances behind him to see if R2-D2 is still watching the live feed over his shoulder but sees instead that R2-D2 is talking with a young woman about how, if this is really the end of the world, wouldn't it be better to spend some time together in the back of an air-conditioned Humvee before running into traffic?

Riles is the first one on the platform getting ready to jump on top of the moving vehicles and a good-sized crowd has gathered to cheer either the success or carnage that is about to happen. The cars aren't going tremendously fast, but as Jimmy watches the aerial feed he cannot imagine being on a platform like that himself, getting ready to jump onto a moving surface. Riles makes his first jump successfully and the crowd puts up more boos than congratulatory cheers and Jimmy is genuinely impressed at how fluidly Riles is able to move his massive, ape-like body across the tops of the cars. He jumps onto the other side of the street and shouts for the next guy on his team to come across.

Jimmy glances behind him and sees R2-D2 and the young woman, or perhaps a different young woman, getting into the back of the Hummer and when he turns back to look at the live stream on the iPad he sees that Team Member 2 has fallen and gotten run over, much to the general delight of the crowd of watchers. Riles comes in over the walkie-talkie and says, "I don't have any other men down here—will it work if we bring one of these civilians with us?" and Jimmy says, "I don't see why not," and Jimmy can see Riles throw his hands up in the air on the Sky Fox feed like "I don't see why not" was not the response he was hoping for. Riles shouts across the street to some of the Gun Pride Thursday cowboy militia and some other people come over and look like they're talking and then Riles says over the walkie-talkie, "Now all these fucks want to kill themselves and I don't have time to stop them," and Jimmy thinks again, briefly, of the girl with the sleeping face and smashed open neck lying in the street.

Chapter Fifteen

Nuclear Physicists Are Not Good with PowerPoint

As some drunken businessmen take turns climbing up on the platform and falling to their deaths into traffic, the Sky Fox live stream shrinks to a small window in the upper left-hand corner of the iPad screen and a red ticker along the bottom of the screen says that there will be a press conference out of New Mexico any minute on developments in the situation and Jimmy wonders if it will be a real press conference or whether any press conferences are real press conferences. There is a podium in front of a blank blue background and a middle-aged bearded man wearing a wrinkled and hastily put together suit steps up and explains that he is a scientist with the University of New Mexico who studies the effects that nuclear testing has had on the state. The scientist motions for someone to join him and a man standing offstage comes on with an easel holding a large butcher paper flip pad, the kind that Jimmy remembered his first grade teacher use to teach the children sight words and was always so much more appealing to Jimmy than the chalk board because the paper made the best thick crinkling sound as his teacher would take each piece in hand and flip it over the top of the pad to reveal a new page. Page one of the butcher paper flip pad reads "1. ATARI CARTRDIGES BURIED IN IRRADIATED SOIL MERGE INTO MEGA CARTRIDGE."

Meanwhile in the Sky Fox feed, Riles and a team of seven or eight others, some military and some civilian, have cleared the second layer and are running toward the third, inner-most layer of the Frogger traffic. No one is saying anything over the walkie-talkie so Jimmy assumes they are probably fine, or as fine as they could be, given the circumstances.

The scientist is on page two of his large butcher paper flip pad display, which reads "2. GIANT CARTRIDGE FLIES, STOPS IN NEAREST MAJOR CITY ON FLIGHT PATH TO REFUEL." He motions his assistant to go to the next page, which reads "3. CARTRIDGE DRAWS POWER FROM CITY, ENACTS GAMES." The scientist explains that they found evidence of four games that could have fed into the giant cartridge—*Centipede, Frogger, Space Invaders*, and *Donkey Kong*—and that they had concluded that the game *E.T. the Extra-Terrestrial* would likely not have been incorporated into the mutant cartridge because that game is just *so awful* that the mega-cartridge would self-destruct if that game was a part of it.

"We've been monitoring the power levels the cartridge is drawing from the city and believe that it's going to run out of power soon," the scientist says. "If we keep engaging it by playing its games, we can hopefully drain its power low enough that it can't fly off again. If we stop playing, we're speculating that it will try to get up and leave for another city where it can continue to draw power and cycle through its games. Of course, this is really all wild speculation." The assistant flips to the fourth major presentation point, which is a series of question marks written in magic marker. "I apologize for the quality of this presentation," the scientist says as he starts to leave the stage. "We had about five minutes to put this together and I'm really no good at PowerPoint. No questions." And then he is gone.

Jimmy hopes that somehow someone is communicating this information to R2-D2, or the skinny guy in the government-controlled construction trailer with all the computer equipment, or to somebody more in control of things than Jimmy and his website stream of Fox News.

The aerial Sky Fox shot takes over the screen again and Jimmy sees that Riles and his makeshift team are nearly all across the third ring of Frogger traffic and he looks up from the screen as the fifth runner, a Gun Pride Thursday cowboy who is the final person needed to beat the *Frogger* level, jumps and lands crookedly on his ankle, then hobbles up and joins the rest of the team. Jimmy can see the logo on the Atari cartridge three blocks away as it sputters and flickers out with the Frogger cars stopping as the *Frogger* logo dies. The *Space Invaders* logo, with the fat, doofy spaceship that looks nothing like the neat little aliens in the game, appears immediately in its place.

Riles, his team, the injured Gun Pride Thursday cowboy, and all the would-be heroes and spectators standing on the sidewalks have no time to react as the cartridge shoots out huge bolts of lightning and uses them to grab the now-stopped *Frogger* cars, lifting them into the air. The cars shake and pulse while they are arranged in a thick blanket over the 16th Street Mall area, with more cars being grabbed and pulled off side streets and parking lots until the field of cars floating above Denver is stacked thick with layers, all vibrating and glowing with energy from the cartridge. And then the beams connecting the cars to the cartridge disappear, and the cars and trucks and vans standing in for the pixilated Space Invader aliens stay suspended above the city, still glowing, and as they begin to sway from side to side Jimmy drops his iPad and walkie-talkie and runs to the Hummer behind him as the first bolts of radioactive energy come blasting out of the cars, destroying the Denver streets below.

Chapter Sixteen

In Which Our Hero Debates Group Sex with R2-D2

Jimmy forces open the door to the backseat of the Hummer and falls face first into R2-D2 being straddled by the still fully-clothed young woman who had followed R2-D2 into the armored vehicle earlier. Jimmy pushes the girl off of R2-D2's wet, unprotected dick and then can't stop staring at R2-D2's wet dick and thinking that this girl was having what could be the last intimate sexual encounter of her life by pushing up her work-appropriate skirt, pulling her panties off to one side, and plopping herself with complete indifference on R2-D2's ready chode. Despite the earth-shaking explosions and screams coming from outside the Hummer, Jimmy's initial impulse to beg R2-D2 for tanks and ground support to shoot the Space Invader aliens down or to tell him that Riles and his team are most likely dead has vacated his mind entirely.

"Well shit," R2-D2 says, "are we going to get weird in here or what?" And the fully-clothed young woman smiles at Jimmy and Jimmy thinks of how he could apply different aspects of cat massage that he has learned from his whisper videos to the body of this fully-clothed young woman and he is surprised that cat massage is the first place he goes when faced with the prospect of actually physically engaging with someone in an intentionally sexual way. He is also surprised, although less so, that the prospect of engaging in some kind of cramped backseat group sex with an older man and an average-at-best-looking woman who seems to have given up entirely has not only immediately made him hard but has also nearly toppled his desire to save the world from the radioactive Atari monster.

"If you don't save the world now," one of the Korean women in the fake lab coats says to Jimmy in his mind, "you won't be able to think back on this encounter and jack off later. And then what's the point?" The other Korean woman standing next to her nods her head. "Who knows," she says as an explosion sends debris into the side of the Hummer, shaking it back and forth. "Maybe you can come back to this when everything's over."

"You're right," Jimmy says, and R2-D2 and the young woman look happy and R2-D2 starts reaching over to Jimmy. "No," Jimmy says, "I mean, no, I don't want to get weird right now. We need to stop the Space Invaders."

R2-D2 leans forward and looks out the tinted window at the bolts of electricity raining down on Denver, starting fires, knocking out sides of buildings, and he says, "Fuck this," opens up the Hummer door, and shoves Jimmy outside. Jimmy looks up at the floating, twitching Space Invader cars in the sky and can see jets zooming above the top layer, shooting down on the cars below.

We need to shoot from the ground up, like in the game, Jimmy thinks, and as R2-D2 grabs the door to slam it shut Jimmy yanks it out of his hands and shouts, "Give me your God damn phone." R2-D2 reaches into his jacket pocket, his erection rapidly declining, and throws his iPhone at Jimmy.

"Good luck saving the world, asshole," R2-D2 says, and as he slams the door shut Jimmy sees the face of the fully-clothed woman one last time, full of both longing and disappointment, an expression that Jimmy often recognizes in himself when he catches his reflection in the bathroom mirror in the mornings.

Chapter Seventeen

In Which Our Hero Battles Space Invaders

Jimmy is huddled in the covered doorframe of a small apartment complex hoping that the next number he tries from R2-D2's contact list connects with somebody from the military, or from whatever shadowy government agency R2-D2 came from, and does not connect with his ex-wife's voicemail or an escort named "Emergency."

"Sir," a frantic voice on the other end says when he picks up, "we thought you were dead. We saw your Hummer get hit." Jimmy can't see R2-D2's Hummer from his current hiding spot and wonders if R2-D2 and the sad, fully-clothed woman really did die fucking. Jimmy wasn't sure about the woman, but he was pretty sure that it was how R2-D2 would have wanted to go.

"This is Jimmy," Jimmy says, realizing immediately after saying it that no one would have any idea who he was. "This is Dr. Turlington," he tries. "The doctor government operative expert. From TV."

"Oh shit," the man on the phone says, "you're that weird pudgy fucker with the sex phone thing who stole my RPG. I have your phone, you know. I saw you on the TV and I was like thank fucking God that your ass didn't die talking to me because you seem like an important motherfucker."

Jimmy feels a swell of energy and adrenaline at the news of his phone and all his saved whisper videos being safe but asks, "Where are you?" instead of asking the SWAT team member about the current condition of his phone.

Fifteen minutes later the SWAT team's armored Hummer pulls up and Jimmy rushes out from his doorframe hiding spot and gets inside. The driver, the SWAT team member who had Jimmy's phone, tells Jimmy that they radioed their military support to tell them to stop with the air assault and get more ground troops out, but the military was being uncooperative and said they'd send in a couple of tanks but really their pilots were pretty excited about this and they didn't want to take that away from them.

The Hummer swerves violently to avoid a falling SUV shot down by a military jet and the SWAT team member continues. "So we put a call out to any other police forces available in the city or anyone else who might have fire power and might be listening to the police channels," he says. As they drive Jimmy sees unarmored police cars and other groups of armed individuals driving up side streets or piling out of vehicles with large weapons ready to fire on the Space Invaders above, and Jimmy is fairly surprised at the number of individuals who both had large weapons available at a moment's notice and their afternoon free to listen to the police channels to hear their call for help. The armored Hummer Jimmy is in is heading directly for the Atari cartridge itself where there seem to be the fewest armed forces, either because they were all blown up if they approached the Atari cartridge earlier or because it was incredibly difficult driving to the thing over all the dead Frogger volunteers in the road.

As they pull up to the cartridge Jimmy is overwhelmed by how huge it is, how sinister the glowing artwork on the front of the cartridge looks, so unlike the images he treasured and traced again and again with his chubby child's fingers when he would examine a game at home. He used to treat each game, each box, each instruction manual like a sacred object, memorizing the colors and shapes and words almost as a form of saying prayers or performing worship. Even though there really wasn't anything he could learn about the gameplay patterns or rhythms necessary to win in competition from the game artifacts themselves, there was something magical about them, about their ability to transform from plastic and metal into a world where he understood the rules and had an honest chance of winning.

There is a ring around the game cartridge itself where the Space Invader cars are not firing, perhaps to avoid hitting the cartridge, Jimmy reasons, but Jimmy stays in the Hummer despite the relative safety of the perimeter they've parked in. From the Hummer's tinted windows Jimmy can see the bodies of the Frogger team that made it to the cartridge— Riles, some men in torn business suits, a Gun Pride Thursday cowboy—as well as the bodies of people who must have been the first to approach the giant when it landed earlier in the day. Jimmy wonders what the final death count will be, whether the 500 deaths on the Fox News counter will wind up being too high or far too low. He wonders if his death will be added into the total, and decides that, even though he does not want to die, it would be nice to have his death be a part of something.

Jimmy climbs into the very back of the Hummer as the SWAT driver and another SWAT team member in the Hummer stand up through the opening in the top of vehicle and fire on the Space Invader cars above. Jimmy half expects the cartridge to shoot their car in retaliation, but he sees the *Space Invaders* logo flicker and is amazed that there has been enough energy available to support the massive amount of cars in the air so far. From his limited viewpoint, he can see other cars in the distance dropping down from the sky and hopes that the SWAT team's call for city-wide backup will actually work.

A fighter jet battling the Space Invader cars from above begins shooting on the cartridge and the cartridge shoots out rays of electricity at the jet, which catches fire and crashes into a Starbucks below. The attack causes several more cars to crash down around Jimmy's Hummer and the *Space Invaders* logo flickers more violently and the cars that came crashing down aren't getting replaced.

"We need to move out of here," Jimmy yells up to the SWAT team members shooting, who either can't hear him or are purposefully ignoring him. "The jets are going to keep attacking the cartridge and it's going to get unpredictable as it starts to die."

"Too much fire farther out," one of the SWAT members shouts down in between gun blasts. Jimmy opens the Hummer door to get a better look at their options for movement and sees another jet, also firing on the cartridge, get blasted by a huge shock of electricity and come barreling straight into the cartridge itself, breaking off a chunk of its upper-right corner. Jimmy slams the door shut and the SWAT members duck back down into the vehicle as sprays of white electricity shoot erratically from the damaged corner of the cartridge. The *Space Invaders* logo on the front of the cartridge turns off, comes back on, turns off again, and about half of the remaining cars still up in the sky rain down as the game glitches.

"We need to go now!" one of the SWAT members says, and as they climb into the front seat a Volkswagen Rabbit smashes into the front end of the Hummer, knocking out the windshield and totaling the car.

"That was lucky," Jimmy says, sprays of electricity from the damaged cartridge still falling around outside the Hummer.

"That was un-fucking-lucky, man," the SWAT driver says. "You see what that did to our car? Now we've got to fucking run through this shit out there. Jesus, what kind of a doctor are you?" And as the three of them get out of the Hummer and start to run the SWAT team member with the contrarian opinions on luck stops Jimmy and says, "Here," and hands Jimmy his phone. There is a crack down the middle and he can't tell if it will turn on but Jimmy smiles and thanks him. "You know," the SWAT member says, "in case we die." And as they start running Jimmy thinks that really what the SWAT member meant was in case we live, because there wouldn't be any point in having the phone if they were to die right now, and Jimmy feels touched that somebody with such a different world view from his own would go out of his way to preserve and carry his phone.

They take shelter under a restaurant awning where several other people are gathered. One of the people, who has his phone out and is taking a video of the scene, screams as his phone dies and man standing next to him slaps him in the face. "Do you really think anyone needs more footage of this shit?" the man says. "Do you think CNN needs another Denver iReporter right now? Shut the fuck up or that thing is gonna hear us."

"It can't hear you," Jimmy says.

"Yeah? You know that for sure, cock suck?" the man says.

"We should go back out there," one of the SWAT guys says to the other. "Take out some more cars. Does it have much longer, you think?" he asks Jimmy.

Jimmy shakes his head no. "It's almost out of juice I think," he says, and he feels like maybe "out of juice" was a lame thing to say, but he's so tired and exhausted and covered in more sweat and blood and grime than he had ever thought possible to have the energy needed to terrorize and second-guess his every action. He wonders if this is what people mean when they say that exercise improves mental health, if people are supposed to work so hard that the idiocy of their lives and thoughts dissipate into a collective pool of exhaustion. More cars are falling out of the sky, and people are shooting into the air all around him, taking out the remaining patches of spazzing Space Invader cars, and Jimmy almost wishes that he, too, had a gun to fire at the cars, even though he wouldn't know how to use it.

The gunfire continues for another few minutes until the last jet that Jimmy can see in the sky does a kamikaze dive into the Atari cartridge, taking out another chunk toward the top and causing the game's power to shut off. Jimmy and the others cowering under the restaurant awning press themselves against the wall of the building, standing shoulder to shoulder as the remaining Space Invader cars fall from the sky, and Jimmy feels closer to these strangers than he has felt to anyone in years.

Chapter Eighteen

The Kill Screen

Cheers begin coming up from the surrounding blocks, hesitantly at first and then with more force as the survivors in the vicinity realize there are no longer flying cars shooting beams of radioactive energy at them. The Atari cartridge's display flickers randomly, as if it can't quite piece together what its next assault might be, and the SWAT guys are high-fiving the people hiding out with Jimmy, and even Jimmy receives a high five, possibly the first of his life, and nobody but Jimmy seems to notice that the cartridge itself is moving and bulging as if a child inside of it is trying to punch its way out onto the 16th Street Mall. The man who was slapped by the other man is saying that he really felt like there was a special moment between them and while Jimmy is aware enough of his surroundings to feel a small sadness that nobody is saying that to him, his primary concern is what the Atari cartridge is doing and whether it might have one last level in it to go.

Jimmy sees the platforms bursting out from within the cartridge and runs toward it with the same blind conviction that led him out of Chuck E. Cheese in the first place, and he knows what the display will read even before it lights up. He shouts for everyone near the game to get back or get inside as he watches one final arm of energy reach out to grab a woman, screaming and still very much alive, and pull her onto the very top of the cartridge as the *Donkey Kong* logo flashes up on the display behind the black crooked rigging platforms that the game has pushed out of itself to create a *Donkey Kong* board. Jimmy is almost to the cartridge and knows that this will be the kill screen, the final level of the game before its programming shorts out and the game is officially over, the stage he never reached at the final tournament he competed at, before the only thing special about him broke. He can feel the cartridge breaking apart inside, like he and the cartridge are connected somehow, and he feels buzzing behind his eyes and through his body like he used to feel when he was close to the end of a game, a feeling that he and the game were the only things that existed. But he knows that they are not the only things to exist and he can hear the woman screaming and he can see her eyes through her wild blowing hair and he knows she can see him running. He only has seven seconds to save the girl before the whole thing blows and he is amazed at how calm he feels.

The cartridge, busting apart from the inside, is glitching. Instead of sending down barrels, fireballs from the level prior to the kill screen are spilling out of the gaping holes in its top and rolling along the platforms jutting out from its surface. Jimmy jumps up on the lowest platform and he knows that this girl is a stranger and that she could be as vapid as White Shorts or as dead inside as R2-D2's fuck buddy and he knows as the seconds tick away that if he's Jumpman in this game scenario he'll die in a matter of moments because Jumpman dies when the game ends, no exceptions. Jimmy's mind feels as clear and confident as it did the first time he held a joystick in his hands, and he is here in this failing kill screen with one direction to go and one goal to move toward: this Pauline at the top of the tower.

Jimmy rushes onto the bottom platform as two fireballs bounce toward him and he jumps onto the first ladder, forcing his sore body up the rungs and feeling the heat of the fireballs beneath him through his thick, black rubber sole Chuck E. Cheese work shoes. Throwing himself up onto the next platform, he barely makes it onto the next ladder before more fireballs swarm the ladder's base. Looking up toward the screaming girl stranded on the top of the cartridge, Jimmy instead sees a final fireball above him, burning in place at the top of the ladder, the same positioning that threw off his pattern recognition as a child. He knows he only has a few seconds left and he knows he might not make it to the top but he also knows he can't fall to the fireballs, not before his time expires.

In the absence of hammers Jimmy recalls a strategy variant believed by some players to be mere superstition: that you can will the fireballs to move based on your movements if you move with confidence and patience. If it looked like you were walking into certain death on one platform, enemies on another platform might back off or change direction, though the lack of certainty about the move made Jimmy unwilling to rely on it in the past. Jimmy wonders if this is why the fireball didn't move out of the way at the tournament so many years before, because he could not handle any deviation from the patterns he had memorized and grown accustomed to. Jimmy stares into the fireball above him and steps down one rung on the ladder, carefully, then another—even though there is something inside of him screaming to keep moving upward toward the girl as the seconds move forward. His feet burn as the flames below begin reaching toward him, and in his half-beat of hesitation he looks into the fireball above him and he has no choice but to believe that it will move, to know that it will move, *and it does*. As the fireball above bounces across the platform and out of Jimmy's way—because he has tricked it by making it look like he is about to step down into the fireballs waiting beneath him—he hurtles himself back up the ladder, taking his one opportunity to escape. Jimmy dashes up to the next platform, only one level below the top of the cartridge. He starts up the final ladder as his seven seconds expires.

The Atari cartridge blows and the force of the explosion shoots Jimmy and the trapped girl into the air. As they fall Jimmy reaches out his hand to catch her but can only reach the tips of her fingers, which feel soft and light as he tries to hold onto them, and he remembers the beautiful random rise and fall of that girl at the arcade when he was seven, her pink nails catching the warm electric light of the games and glinting as they went up and down her companion's shoulder. He thinks that if this is the last thing he imagines—the small movements of that girl's hand so long ago—and if this is the last thing that he feels—this girl's fingertips pressed against his as they fall—then it was worth it. Getting past the fireballs and making it through the kill screen was worth it, even if it was just to die.

Jimmy tastes the blood pooling in his mouth and though he isn't sure he can move he turns his eyes to see a blurry vision of the girl lying next to him and he realizes that he and the girl have landed on the piles of dead bodies that have been accumulating around the Atari cartridge all day. The girl's eyes are open and conscious but dazed, and Jimmy feels a tingling in his crotch, which he hopes means his spine isn't severed, and he says, "Hello, my name is Jimmy," and the Korean women in his mind applaud wildly and the girl coughs up some blood and says, "Nice to meet you," and Jimmy feels happier about not being dead than he ever has felt in his entire life. He thinks of what his old rival had said at the end of the Donkey Kong tournament, that you can't beat the game, that the game just ends. As a child it had seemed so devastating that the champion wasn't real, that he was just the person that kept moving forward the longest, but as Jimmy blinks his eyes and brings the girl lying next to him into focus, the thought fills him with relief.

Amanda Billings received her MFA from Colorado State University, where she works as an instructor and advisor. Her work has appeared in *Lamination Colony*, *Bust Down the Door and Eat All the Chickens*, *Cream City Review*, and *A Poetic Inventory of Rocky Mountain National Park*, among others. She lives with her husband in Fort Collins, Colorado.

BIZARRO BOOKS

CATALOG   SPRING 2013

ERASERHEAD
PRESS

Your major resource for the bizarro fiction genre:

WWW.BIZARROCENTRAL.COM

Introduce yourselves to the bizarro fiction genre and all of its authors with the Bizarro Starter Kit series. Each volume features short novels and short stories by ten of the leading bizarro authors, designed to give you a perfect sampling of the genre for only $10.

BB-0X1
"The Bizarro Starter Kit" (Orange)
Featuring D. Harlan Wilson, Carlton Mellick III, Jeremy Robert Johnson, Kevin L Donihe, Gina Ranalli, Andre Duza, Vincent W. Sakowski, Steve Beard, John Edward Lawson, and Bruce Taylor.
236 pages $10

BB-0X2
"The Bizarro Starter Kit" (Blue)
Featuring Ray Fracalossy, Jeremy C. Shipp, Jordan Krall, Mykle Hansen, Andersen Prunty, Eckhard Gerdes, Bradley Sands, Steve Aylett, Christian TeBordo, and Tony Rauch. **244 pages $10**

BB-0X2
"The Bizarro Starter Kit" (Purple)
Featuring Russell Edson, Athena Villaverde, David Agranoff, Matthew Revert, Andrew Goldfarb, Jeff Burk, Garrett Cook, Kris Saknussemm, Cody Goodfellow, and Cameron Pierce **264 pages $10**

BB-001"The Kafka Effekt" D. Harlan Wilson — A collection of forty-four irreal short stories loosely written in the vein of Franz Kafka, with more than a pinch of William S. Burroughs sprinkled on top. 211 pages $14

BB-002 "Satan Burger" Carlton Mellick III — The cult novel that put Carlton Mellick III on the map ... Six punks get jobs at a fast food restaurant owned by the devil in a city violently overpopulated by surreal alien cultures. 236 pages $14

BB-003 "Some Things Are Better Left Unplugged" Vincent Sakwoski — Join The Man and his Nemesis, the obese tabby, for a nightmare roller coaster ride into this postmodern fantasy. 152 pages $10

BB-005 "Razor Wire Pubic Hair" Carlton Mellick III — A genderless humandildo is purchased by a razor dominatrix and brought into her nightmarish world of bizarre sex and mutilation. 176 pages $11

BB-007 "The Baby Jesus Butt Plug" Carlton Mellick III — Using clones of the Baby Jesus for anal sex will be the hip sex fetish of the future. 92 pages $10

BB-010 "The Menstruating Mall" Carlton Mellick III — "The Breakfast Club meets Chopping Mall as directed by David Lynch." - Brian Keene 212 pages $12

BB-011 "Angel Dust Apocalypse" Jeremy Robert Johnson — Meth-heads, man-made monsters, and murderous Neo-Nazis. "Seriously amazing short stories..." - Chuck Palahniuk, author of Fight Club 184 pages $11

BB-015 "Foop!" Chris Genoa — Strange happenings are going on at Dactyl, Inc, the world's first and only time travel tourism company.
"A surreal pie in the face!" - Christopher Moore 300 pages $14

BB-032 **"Extinction Journals" Jeremy Robert Johnson** — An uncanny voyage across a newly nuclear America where one man must confront the problems associated with loneliness, insane dieties, radiation, love, and an ever-evolving cockroach suit with a mind of its own. **104 pages $10**

BB-037 **"The Haunted Vagina" Carlton Mellick III** — It's difficult to love a woman whose vagina is a gateway to the world of the dead. **132 pages $10**

BB-043 **"War Slut" Carlton Mellick III** — Part "1984," part "Waiting for Godot," and part action horror video game adaptation of John Carpenter's "The Thing." **116 pages $10**

BB-047 **"Sausagey Santa" Carlton Mellick III** — A bizarro Christmas tale featuring Santa as a piratey mutant with a body made of sausages. 124 pages $10

BB-048 **"Misadventures in a Thumbnail Universe" Vincent Sakowski** — Dive deep into the surreal and satirical realms of neo-classical Blender Fiction, filled with television shoes and flesh-filled skies. **120 pages $10**

BB-053 **"Ballad of a Slow Poisoner" Andrew Goldfarb** — Millford Mutterwurst sat down on a Tuesday to take his afternoon tea, and made the unpleasant discovery that his elbows were becoming flatter. **128 pages $10**

BB-055 **"Help! A Bear is Eating Me" Mykle Hansen** — The bizarro, heartwarming, magical tale of poor planning, hubris and severe blood loss... **150 pages $11**

BB-056 **"Piecemeal June" Jordan Krall** — A man falls in love with a living sex doll, but with love comes danger when her creator comes after her with crab-squid assassins. **90 pages $9**

BB-058 **"The Overwhelming Urge" Andersen Prunty** — A collection of bizarro tales by Andersen Prunty. **150 pages $11**

BB-059 **"Adolf in Wonderland" Carlton Mellick III** — A dreamlike adventure that takes a young descendant of Adolf Hitler's design and sends him down the rabbit hole into a world of imperfection and disorder. **180 pages $11**

BB-061 **"Ultra Fuckers" Carlton Mellick III** — Absurdist suburban horror about a couple who enter an upper middle class gated community but can't find their way out. **108 pages $9**

BB-062 **"House of Houses" Kevin L. Donihe** — An odd man wants to marry his house. Unfortunately, all of the houses in the world collapse at the same time in the Great House Holocaust. Now he must travel to House Heaven to find his departed fiancee. **172 pages $11**

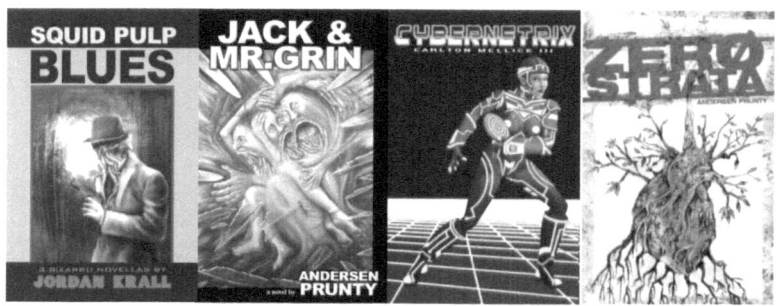

BB-064 **"Squid Pulp Blues" Jordan Krall** — In these three bizarro-noir novellas, the reader is thrown into a world of murderers, drugs made from squid parts, deformed gun-toting veterans, and a mischievous apocalyptic donkey. **204 pages $12**

BB-065 **"Jack and Mr. Grin" Andersen Prunty** — "When Mr. Grin calls you can hear a smile in his voice. Not a warm and friendly smile, but the kind that seizes your spine in fear. You don't need to pay your phone bill to hear it. That smile is in every line of Prunty's prose." - Tom Bradley. **208 pages $12**

BB-066 **"Cybernetrix" Carlton Mellick III** — What would you do if your normal everyday world was slowly mutating into the video game world from Tron? **212 pages $12**

BB-072 **"Zerostrata" Andersen Prunty** — Hansel Nothing lives in a tree house, suffers from memory loss, has a very eccentric family, and falls in love with a woman who runs naked through the woods every night. **144 pages $11**

BB-073 **"The Egg Man" Carlton Mellick III** — It is a world where humans reproduce like insects. Children are the property of corporations, and having an enormous ten-foot brain implanted into your skull is a grotesque sexual fetish. Mellick's industrial urban dystopia is one of his darkest and grittiest to date. **184 pages $11**

BB-074 **"Shark Hunting in Paradise Garden" Cameron Pierce** — A group of strange humanoid religious fanatics travel back in time to the Garden of Eden to discover it is invested with hundreds of giant flying maneating sharks. **150 pages $10**

BB-075 **"Apeshit" Carlton Mellick III** - Friday the 13th meets Visitor Q. Six hipster teens go to a cabin in the woods inhabited by a deformed killer. An incredibly fucked-up parody of B-horror movies with a bizarro slant. **192 pages $12**

BB-076 **"Fuckers of Everything on the Crazy Shitting Planet of the Vomit At smosphere" Mykle Hansen** - Three bizarro satires. Monster Cocks, Journey to the Center of Agnes Cuddlebottom, and Crazy Shitting Planet. **228 pages $12**

BB-077 **"The Kissing Bug" Daniel Scott Buck** — In the tradition of Roald Dahl, Tim Burton, and Edward Gorey, comes this bizarro anti-war children's story about a bohemian conenose kissing bug who falls in love with a human woman. **116 pages $10**

BB-078 **"MachoPoni" Lotus Rose** — It's My Little Pony... *Bizarro* style! A long time ago Poniworld was split in two. On one side of the Jagged Line is the Pastel Kingdom, a magical land of music, parties, and positivity. On the other side of the Jagged Line is Dark Kingdom inhabited by an army of undead ponies. **148 pages $11**

BB-079 **"The Faggiest Vampire" Carlton Mellick III** — A Roald Dahl-esque children's story about two faggy vampires who partake in a mustache competition to find out which one is truly the faggiest. **104 pages $10**

BB-080 **"Sky Tongues" Gina Ranalli** — The autobiography of Sky Tongues, the biracial hermaphrodite actress with tongues for fingers. Follow her strange life story as she rises from freak to fame. **204 pages $12**

BB-081 **"Washer Mouth" Kevin L. Donihe** - A washing machine becomes human and pursues his dream of meeting his favorite soap opera star. **244 pages $11**

BB-082 **"Shatnerquake" Jeff Burk** - All of the characters ever played by William Shatner are suddenly sucked into our world. Their mission: hunt down and destroy the real William Shatner. **100 pages $10**

BB-083 **"The Cannibals of Candyland" Carlton Mellick III** - There exists a race of cannibals that are made of candy. They live in an underground world made out of candy. One man has dedicated his life to killing them all. **170 pages $11**

BB-084 **"Slub Glub in the Weird World of the Weeping Willows"** **Andrew Goldfarb** - The charming tale of a blue glob named Slub Glub who helps the weeping willows whose tears are flooding the earth. There are also hyenas, ghosts, and a voodoo priest **100 pages $10**

BB-085 **"Super Fetus" Adam Pepper** - Try to abort this fetus and he'll kick your ass! **104 pages $10**

BB-086 **"Fistful of Feet" Jordan Krall** - A bizarro tribute to spaghetti westerns, featuring Cthulhu-worshipping Indians, a woman with four feet, a crazed gunman who is obsessed with sucking on candy, Syphilis-ridden mutants, sexually transmitted tattoos, and a house devoted to the freakiest fetishes. **228 pages $12**

BB-087 **"Ass Goblins of Auschwitz" Cameron Pierce** - It's Monty Python meets Nazi exploitation in a surreal nightmare as can only be imagined by Bizarro author Cameron Pierce. **104 pages $10**

BB-088 **"Silent Weapons for Quiet Wars" Cody Goodfellow** - "This is high-end psychological surrealist horror meets bottom-feeding low-life crime in a techno-thrilling science fiction world full of Lovecraft and magic..." -John Skipp **212 pages $12**

BB-089 **"Warrior Wolf Women of the Wasteland" Carlton Mellick III**
— Road Warrior Werewolves versus McDonaldland Mutants...post-apocalyptic fiction has never been quite like this. **316 pages $13**

BB-091 **"Super Giant Monster Time" Jeff Burk** — A tribute to choose your own adventures and Godzilla movies. Will you escape the giant monsters that are rampaging the fuck out of your city and shit? Or will you join the mob of alien-controlled punk rockers causing chaos in the streets? What happens next depends on you. **188 pages $12**

BB-092 **"Perfect Union" Cody Goodfellow** — "Cronenberg's THE FLY on a grand scale: human/insect gene-spliced body horror, where the human hive politics are as shocking as the gore." -John Skipp. **272 pages $13**

BB-093 **"Sunset with a Beard" Carlton Mellick III** — 14 stories of surreal science fiction. **200 pages $12**

BB-094 **"My Fake War" Andersen Prunty** — The absurd tale of an unlikely soldier forced to fight a war that, quite possibly, does not exist. It's Rambo meets Waiting for Godot in this subversive satire of American values and the scope of the human imagination. **128 pages $11**

BB-095 **"Lost in Cat Brain Land" Cameron Pierce** — Sad stories from a surreal world. A fascist mustache, the ghost of Franz Kafka, a desert inside a dead cat. Primordial entities mourn the death of their child. The desperate serve tea to mysterious creatures. A hopeless romantic falls in love with a pterodactyl. And much more. **152 pages $11**

BB-096 **"The Kobold Wizard's Dildo of Enlightenment +2" Carlton Mellick III** — A Dungeons and Dragons parody about a group of people who learn they are only made up characters in an AD&D campaign and must find a way to resist their nerdy teenaged players and retarded dungeon master in order to survive. 232 **pages $12**

BB-098 **"A Hundred Horrible Sorrows of Ogner Stump" Andrew Goldfarb** — Goldfarb's acclaimed comic series. A magical and weird journey into the horrors of everyday life. **164 pages $11**

BB-099 **"Pickled Apocalypse of Pancake Island" Cameron Pierce**—A demented fairy tale about a pickle, a pancake, and the apocalypse. **102 pages $8**

BB-100 **"Slag Attack" Andersen Prunty**— Slag Attack features four visceral, noir stories about the living, crawling apocalypse.A slag is what survivors are calling the slug-like maggots raining·from the sky, burrowing inside people, and hollowing out their flesh and their sanity. **148 pages $11**

BB-101 **"Slaughterhouse High" Robert Devereaux**—A place where schools are built with secret passageways, rebellious teens get zippers installed in their mouths and genitals, and once a year, on that special night, one couple is slaughtered and the bits of their bodies are kept as souvenirs. **304 pages $13**

BB-102 **"The Emerald Burrito of Oz" John Skipp & Marc Levinthal** —OZ IS REAL! Magic is real! The gate is really in Kansas! And America is finally allowing Earth tourists to visit this weird-ass, mysterious land. But when Gene of Los Angeles heads off for summer vacation in the Emerald City, little does he know that a war is brewing...a war that could destroy both worlds. **280 pages $13**

BB-103 **"The Vegan Revolution... with Zombies" David Agranoff** — When there's no more meat in hell, the vegans will walk the earth. **160 pages $11**

BB-104 **"The Flappy Parts" Kevin L Donihe**—Poems about bunnies, LSD, and police abuse. You know, things that matter. **132 pages $11**

BB-105 **"Sorry I Ruined Your Orgy" Bradley Sands**—Bizarro humorist Bradley Sands returns with one of the strangest, most hilarious collections of the year. **130 pages $11**

BB-106 **"Mr. Magic Realism" Bruce Taylor**—Like Golden Age science fiction comics written by Freud, *Mr. Magic Realism* is a strange, insightful adventure that spans the furthest reaches of the galaxy, exploring the hidden caverns in the hearts and minds of men, women, aliens, and biomechanical cats. **152 pages $11**

BB-107 **"Zombies and Shit" Carlton Mellick III**—"Battle Royale" meets "Return of the Living Dead." Mellick's bizarro tribute to the zombie genre. **308 pages $13**

BB-108 **"The Cannibal's Guide to Ethical Living" Mykle Hansen**— Over a five star French meal of fine wine, organic vegetables and human flesh, a lunatic delivers a witty, chilling, disturbingly sane argument in favor of eating the rich.. **184 pages $11**

BB-109 **"Starfish Girl" Athena Villaverde**—In a post-apocalyptic underwater dome society, a girl with a starfish growing from her head and an assassin with sea anenome hair are on the run from a gang of mutant fish men. **160 pages $11**

BB-110 **"Lick Your Neighbor" Chris Genoa**—Mutant ninjas, a talking whale, kung fu masters, maniacal pilgrims, and an alcoholic clown populate Chris Genoa's surreal, darkly comical and unnerving reimagining of the first Thanksgiving. **303 pages $13**

BB-111 **"Night of the Assholes" Kevin L. Donihe**—A plague of assholes is infecting the countryside. Normal everyday people are transforming into jerks, snobs, dicks, and douchebags. And they all have only one purpose: to make your life a living hell.. **192 pages $11**

BB-112 **"Jimmy Plush, Teddy Bear Detective" Garrett Cook**—Hardboiled cases of a private detective trapped within a teddy bear body. **180 pages $11**

BB-113 **"The Deadheart Shelters" Forrest Armstrong**—The hip hop lovechild of William Burroughs and Dali... **144 pages $11**

BB-114 **"Eyeballs Growing All Over Me... Again" Tony Raugh**— Absurd, surreal, playful, dream-like, whimsical, and a lot of fun to read. **144 pages $11**

BB-115 **"Whargoul" Dave Brockie** — From the killing grounds of Stalingrad to the death camps of the holocaust. From torture chambers in Iraq to race riots in the United States, the Whargoul was there, killing and raping. **244 pages $12**

BB-116 **"By the Time We Leave Here, We'll Be Friends" J. David Osborne** — A David Lynchian nightmare set in a Russian gulag, where its prisoners, guards, traitors, soldiers, lovers, and demons fight for survival and their own rapidly deteriorating humanity. **168 pages $11**

BB-117 **"Christmas on Crack" edited by Carlton Mellick III** — Perverted Christmas Tales for the whole family! . . . as long as every member of your family is over the age of 18. **168 pages $11**

BB-118 **"Crab Town" Carlton Mellick III** — Radiation fetishists, balloon people, mutant crabs, sail-bike road warriors, and a love affair between a woman and an H-Bomb. This is one mean asshole of a city. Welcome to Crab Town. **100 pages $8**

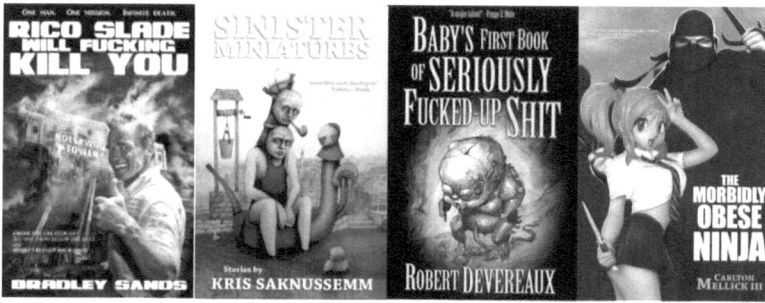

BB-119 **"Rico Slade Will Fucking Kill You" Bradley Sands** — Rico Slade is an action hero. Rico Slade can rip out a throat with his bare hands. Rico Slade's favorite food is the honey-roasted peanut. Rico Slade will fucking kill everyone. A novel. **122 pages $8**

BB-120 **"Sinister Miniatures" Kris Saknussemm** — The definitive collection of short fiction by Kris Saknussemm, confirming that he is one of the best, most daring writers of the weird to emerge in the twenty-first century. **180 pages $11**

BB-121 **"Baby's First Book of Seriously Fucked up Shit" Robert Devereaux** — Ten stories of the strange, the gross, and the just plain fucked up from one of the most original voices in horror. **176 pages $11**

BB-122 **"The Morbidly Obese Ninja" Carlton Mellick III** — These days, if you want to run a successful company . . . you're going to need a lot of ninjas. **92 pages $8**

BB-123 **"Abortion Arcade" Cameron Pierce**— An intoxicating blend of body horror and midnight movie madness, reminiscent of early David Lynch and the splatterpunks at their most sublime. **172 pages $11**

BB-124 **"Black Hole Blues" Patrick Wensink** — A hilarious double helix of country music and physics. **196 pages $11**

BB-125 **"Barbarian Beast Bitches of the Badlands" Carlton Mellick III** — Three prequels and sequels to *Warrior Wolf Women of the Wasteland*. **284 pages $13**

BB-126 **"The Traveling Dildo Salesman" Kevin L. Donihe** — A nightmare comedy about destiny, faith, and sex toys. Also featuring Donihe's most lurid and infamous short stories: *Milky Agitation, Two-Way Santa, The Helen Mower, Living Room Zombies,* and *Revenge of the Living Masturbation Rag.* **108 pages $8**

BB-127 **"Metamorphosis Blues" Bruce Taylor** — Enter a land of love beasts, intergalactic cowboys, and rock 'n roll. A land where Sears Catalogs are doorways to insanity and men keep mysterious black boxes. Welcome to the monstrous mind of Mr. Magic Realism. **136 pages $11**

BB-128 **"The Driver's Guide to Hitting Pedestrians" Andersen Prunty** — A pocket guide to the twenty-three most painful things in life, written by the most well-adjusted man in the universe. **108 pages $8**

BB-129 **"Island of the Super People" Kevin Shamel** — Four students and their anthropology professor journey to a remote island to study its indigenous population. But this is no ordinary native culture. They're super heroes and villains with flesh costumes and out-landish abilities like self-detonation, musical eyelashes, and microwave hands. **194 pages $11**

BB-130 **"Fantastic Orgy" Carlton Mellick III** — Shark Sex, mutant cats, and strange sexually transmitted diseases. Featuring the stories: *Candy-coated, Ear Cat, Fantastic Orgy, City Hobgoblins,* and *Porno in August.* **136 pages $9**

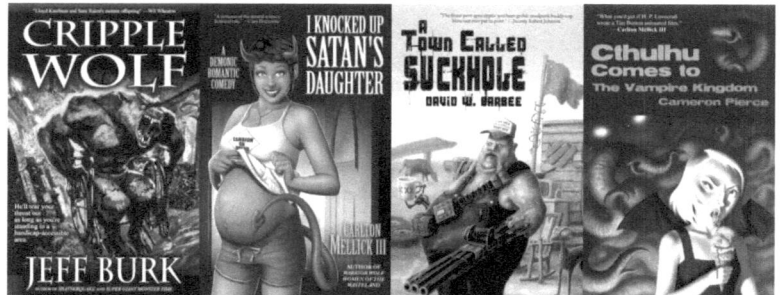

BB-131 **"Cripple Wolf" Jeff Burk** — Part man. Part wolf. 100% crippled. Also including *Punk Rock Nursing Home, Adrift with Space Badgers, Cook for Your Life, Just Another Day in the Park, Frosty and the Full Monty*, and *House of Cats*. **152 pages $10**

BB-132 **"I Knocked Up Satan's Daughter" Carlton Mellick III** — An adorable, violent, fantastical love story. A romantic comedy for the bizarro fiction reader. **152 pages $10**

BB-133 **"A Town Called Suckhole" David W. Barbee** — Far into the future, in the nuclear bowels of post-apocalyptic Dixie, there is a town. A town of derelict mobile homes, ancient junk, and mutant wildlife. A town of slack jawed rednecks who bask in the splendors of moonshine and mud boggin'. A town dedicated to the bloody and demented legacy of the Old South. A town called Suckhole. **144 pages $10**

BB-134 **"Cthulhu Comes to the Vampire Kingdom" Cameron Pierce** — What you'd get if H. P. Lovecraft wrote a Tim Burton animated film. **148 pages $11**

BB-135 **"I am Genghis Cum" Violet LeVoit** — From the savage Arctic tundra to post-partum mutations to your missing daughter's unmarked grave, join visionary madwoman Violet LeVoit in this non-stop eight-story onslaught of full-tilt Bizarro punk lit thrills. **124 pages $9**

BB-136 **"Haunt" Laura Lee Bahr** — A tripping-balls Los Angeles noir, where a mysterious dame drags you through a time-warping Bizarro hall of mirrors. **316 pages $13**

BB-137 **"Amazing Stories of the Flying Spaghetti Monster" edited by Cameron Pierce** — Like an all-spaghetti evening of Adult Swim, the Flying Spaghetti Monster will show you the many realms of His Noodly Appendage. Learn of those who worship him and the lives he touches in distant, mysterious ways. **228 pages $12**

BB-138 **"Wave of Mutilation" Douglas Lain** — A dream-pop exploration of modern architecture and the American identity, *Wave of Mutilation* is a Zen finger trap for the 21st century. **100 pages $8**

BB-139 **"Hooray for Death!" Mykle Hansen** — Famous Author Mykle Hansen draws unconventional humor from deaths tiny and large, and invites you to laugh while you can. **128 pages $10**

BB-140 **"Hypno-hog's Moonshine Monster Jamboree" Andrew Goldfarb** — Hicks, Hogs, Horror! Goldfarb is back with another strange illustrated tale of backwoods weirdness. **120 pages $9**

BB-141 **"Broken Piano For President" Patrick Wensink** — A comic masterpiece about the fast food industry, booze, and the necessity to choose happiness over work and security. **372 pages $15**

BB-142 **"Please Do Not Shoot Me in the Face" Bradley Sands** — A novel in three parts, *Please Do Not Shoot Me in the Face: A Novel*, is the story of one boy detective, the worst ninja in the world, and the great American fast food wars. It is a novel of loss, destruction, and--incredibly--genuine hope. **224 pages $12**

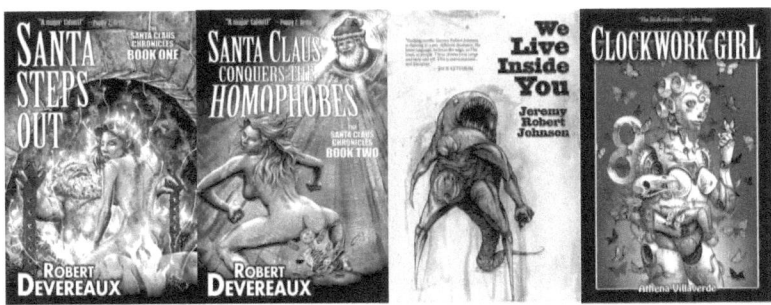

BB-143 **"Santa Steps Out" Robert Devereaux** — Sex, Death, and Santa Claus ... The ultimate erotic Christmas story is back. **294 pages $13**

BB-144 **"Santa Conquers the Homophobes" Robert Devereaux** — "I wish I could hope to ever attain one-thousandth the perversity of Robert Devereaux's toenail clippings." - Poppy Z. Brite **316 pages $13**

BB-145 **"We Live Inside You" Jeremy Robert Johnson** — "Jeremy Robert Johnson is dancing to a way different drummer. He loves language, he loves the edge, and he loves us people. These stories have range and style and wit. This is entertainment... and literature."- Jack Ketchum **188 pages $11**

BB-146 **"Clockwork Girl" Athena Villaverde** — Urban fairy tales for the weird girl in all of us. Like a combination of Francesca Lia Block, Charles de Lint, Kathe Koja, Tim Burton, and Hayao Miyazaki, her stories are cute, kinky, edgy, magical, provocative, and strange, full of poetic imagery and vicious sexuality. **160 pages $10**

BB-147 **"Armadillo Fists" Carlton Mellick III** — A weird-as-hell gangster story set in a world where people drive giant mechanical dinosaurs instead of cars. **168 pages $11**

BB-148 **"Gargoyle Girls of Spider Island" Cameron Pierce** — Four college seniors venture out into open waters for the tropical party weekend of a lifetime. Instead of a teenage sex fantasy, they find themselves in a nightmare of pirates, sharks, and sex-crazed monsters. **100 pages $8**

BB-149 **"The Handsome Squirm" by Carlton Mellick III** — Like Franz Kafka's *The Trial* meets an erotic body horror version of *The Blob*. **158 pages $11**

BB-150 **"Tentacle Death Trip" Jordan Krall** — It's *Death Race 2000* meets H. P. Lovecraft in bizarro author Jordan Krall's best and most suspenseful work to date. **224 pages $12**

BB-151 **"The Obese" Nick Antosca** — Like Alfred Hitchcock's *The Birds*... but with obese people. **108 pages $10**

BB-152 **"All-Monster Action!" Cody Goodfellow** — The world gave him a blank check and a demand: Create giant monsters to fight our wars. But Dr. Otaku was not satisfied with mere chaos and mass destruction.... **216 pages $12**

BB-153 **"Ugly Heaven" Carlton Mellick III** — Heaven is no longer a paradise. It was once a blissful utopia full of wonders far beyond human comprehension. But the afterlife is now in ruins. It has become an ugly, lonely wasteland populated by strange monstrous beasts, masturbating angels, and sad man-like beings wallowing in the remains of the once-great Kingdom of God. **106 pages $8**

BB-154 **"Space Walrus" Kevin L. Donihe** — Walter is supposed to go where no walrus has ever gone before, but all this astronaut walrus really wants is to take it easy on the intense training, escape the chimpanzee bullies, and win the love of his human trainer Dr. Stephanie. **160 pages $11**

BB-155 **"Unicorn Battle Squad" Kirsten Alene** — Mutant unicorns. A palace with a thousand human legs. The most powerful army on the planet. **192 pages $11**

BB-156 **"Kill Ball" Carlton Mellick III** — In a city where all humans live inside of plastic bubbles, exotic dancers are being murdered in the rubbery streets by a mysterious stalker known only as Kill Ball. **134 pages $10**

BB-157 **"Die You Doughnut Bastards" Cameron Pierce** — The bacon storm is rolling in. We hear the grease and sugar beat against the roof and windows. The doughnut people are attacking. We press close together, forgetting for a moment that we hate each other. **196 pages $11**

BB-158 **"Tumor Fruit" Carlton Mellick III** — Eight desperate castaways find themselves stranded on a mysterious deserted island. They are surrounded by poisonous blue plants and an ocean made of acid. Ravenous creatures lurk in the toxic jungle. The ghostly sound of crying babies can be heard on the wind. **310 pages $13**

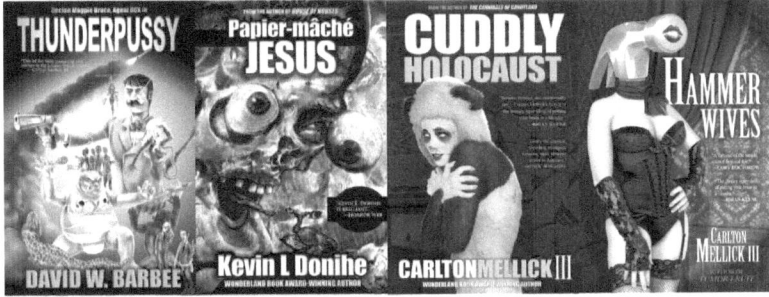

BB-159 **"Thunderpussy" David W. Barbee** — When it comes to high-tech global espionage, only one man has the balls to save humanity from the world's most powerful bastards. He's Declan Magpie Bruce, Agent 00X. **136 pages $11**

BB-160 **"Papier Mâché Jesus" Kevin L. Donihe** — Donihe's surreal wit and beautiful mind-bending imagination is on full display with stories such as All Children Go to Hell, Happiness is a Warm Gun, and Swimming in Endless Night. **154 pages $11**

BB-161 **"Cuddly Holocaust" Carlton Mellick III** — The war between humans and toys has come to an end. The toys won. **172 pages $11**

BB-162 **"Hammer Wives" Carlton Mellick III** — Fish-eyed mutants, oceans of insects, and flesh-eating women with hammers for heads. Hammer Wives collects six of his most popular novelettes and short stories. **152 pages $10**